PARISH

a sequel to Freakhouse

ASHLEY NEWELL

For more information about the author and up-coming books, please visit www.newellbooks.com

ISBN: 1539391663
ISBN-13: 978-1539391661

AUTHOR'S NOTE

When I committed to write *Freakhouse* for NaNoWriMo, I knew that Dotan would guide me through it in all its detail. He didn't disappoint. But when we reached Blue's scene in the stairwell, my fearless leader started to shut down. The timing couldn't have been worse! I still had to write the story and I was nowhere near the finish mark, but I could feel Dotan shutting me out.

I do talk about characters as though they are real, because when you live inside of their world for however long, you understand that the story you're telling is theirs, not yours. The thought of losing Blue ripped out my heart, and I could see how it destroyed Dotan. I tried to compromise. I tried to think of how to avoid it, but it was like a fixed event in time. Blue had to see Dotan and Jos together – it was the only way for Dotan to finally grow up. Still, I couldn't very well survive NaNoWriMo with my narrator on strike. It had to be done, *Freakhouse* had to end this way. I would write it with or without him!

Unfortunately I just couldn't invest in the story without knowing what was to become of Dotan. I don't believe that writers always need to supply an epilogue that tells you what happened fifty years down the road and who their grandchildren married. I do, however, believe that it is important to know for yourself what happened, even if you omit it on the page. I needed to know. I needed to know if it destroyed him. I needed to know what the consequences of this near escape were. I needed to know if anyone had a future after this.

I don't know how many days it took. Might have been weeks for all I know. I started toying with a few ideas, just testing them out, much like I had done in realizing Dotan as a character in the first place. I threw a seemingly nonsensical idea out into the universe, not expecting so much as an echo. But it wasn't an echo that responded. It was Dotan. "Now you're getting it," he seemed to say.

I didn't know if I wanted to write this part of the story, and more than that, I didn't know if I wanted to share it. But this is the other half. This is the part that Dotan forced me to discover on my own. He's finicky like that.

So hang on tight, everyone. We're going back in.

Lead the way, Dotan...

- Ashley Newell

For all those who, like me,
are still crying on the parkade floor.

1

TASTE OF PAVEMENT

"Halt! You are in a restricted area. Remain where you are. You are in a restricted area. Remain where you are. Attendants will assist you shortly. Halt! You are in a restricted area. Remain where you are."

The wind is knocked out of me as they shove my chest into the glass-covered concrete. I know that somewhere within me I realize that this hurts like hell, but right now all I feel is relief. Jos got away in his car. That last sliver of sunlight has been stomped out probably forever. I don't know what they're going to do with me now, but whatever it is, I don't regret this part. They can't hurt me now. Whatever the punishment is for Freaks, I'll take it; I deserve it.

My arms are twisted behind my back. Something pops. I think it's my elbow. I'll figure out how bad it is later. I might as well wait to deal with this whole reality once they've finally finished with me. I keep my eyes fixed on that garage door as best as I can.

Someone pushes my face down, a bulky knee grinding into my jaw.

My arms are pinched. Tight restraints clamp down on my wrists.

I can't move, not that I'm even trying to. Now it's hard to

see much more than the glinting shards of rear window glass. This close to the ground, the shards look more like stones, rough-cut gem stones scattered over the ground of this dark cavern. They have a dull tint in the poor garage lighting. It's like someone put in a blue gel over one of the lights above me.

It makes my eyes sting. Even in my own head I want to say that it's just the beating that I'm getting, it's the dirt being kicked up, it's anything but what I feel in the pit of my stomach.

I don't wish it away. I doubt that Blue... Zac... I doubt he felt any comfort in his last moments, hitting each steel step as his convulsions overpowered his body, as complete and utter heartbreak overwhelmed him. *Hit me again.* I don't deserve to get off this easy. I open my eyes despite the sting.

My face is being squished down harder. I can't see it, but I can hear the attendants around me quickly shuffle back. They've moved just enough to let someone else in. I can imagine well enough the White Coat who's going to stick me.

The sharp jab in the side of my neck makes me involuntarily grunt but I don't resist it. The amount of force that they're using to hold me down is completely pointless. I would have walked right back in on my own accord if I had to. I want them to take me back. I want them to take me home. However much *home* I have left to go back to.

"Don't leave me," he said to me, cradled in my arms.

I had promised him then, and like an asshole I betrayed him. I let him go just for one stupid moment with Jos that I should never have let happen. If ever I had the power to undo something...

I'm feeling heavier. My sedation is setting in. My blurred vision can hardly distinguish basic shapes anymore, but I can still see the colours. The black. The glinting blue.

"Don't leave me." I can still hear him. I can still feel him.

"I'm right here."

2

IN & OUT

I feel it now. My whole body feels smashed up and useless. My eyes can barely open. It hurts just to try. I can't see anything. Everything is a haze. Even my ears feel clogged up. I can hear some sound, but it's so muffled and distant, like trying to listen underwater. It hurts to try. It all just hurts.

Something releases from within me. Salty tears burn my eyes.

I give up.

I hear the sounds first. Underwater, but as I gain more feeling, the noises get sharper, more distinct. I can hear the buzzing and beeping of the equipment. Tapping. Doors opening and closing. Shoes treading. A cough. Mumbled conversation.

My face is still tender and my eyelids sore, but I feel the desperate need to open them. I have the strange feeling that they've been closed for far too long. Based on how difficult a feat it is, and by how much gunk of both the gooey and crusty variety I feel, I know that I've been out, and deeply, for who knows how long.

I instinctively try to wipe my eyes clean, but I can't. My

arms are strapped down; so is my chest; and both the upper and lower parts of my legs. I keep forgetting that I'm considered dangerous. Even before my escape attempt I was monitored as if I were a ticking time bomb.

Escape. Ha. As if it could even be called that. It's a stupid word to think of. I surrendered. I turned back. It wasn't much of an escape. It wasn't even much of an attempt. Another one of Jos's brilliant ideas of doing things for *my* sake. Screw my sake. He's better off without me. So am I. There isn't anywhere out there in the "real" world that's worth getting to. I don't miss it. I'm determined that I won't even miss Jos. I forgot to miss him once before; I can easily do that again.

My crusty eyes show me what I already guessed. I'm in a Doc's office, a small space much like Dr. Isaacs's, only less cluttered and more sterile looking. I can see the lonely desk in the corner. The top shelving is practically empty and the desk is bare except for a charger stand, probably for one of the trusty tablets every White Coat carries around.

I wriggle as best as I can, just to try to get a better view of my surroundings, but I'm locked in here pretty tight. The door is hidden to me. It seems like there must be a closet or something that juts into the room, the door hidden by this intrusion of a block of wall. There are no windows from what I can tell.

The door opens again. The soft tap of rubber-soled shoes on the cold floor come closer to me. I turn my head as best as I can. It's a White Coat, a woman, young, clutching onto her tablet tight against her chest; I can't even see her badge. Another White Coat woman comes in from behind her, older, looser in her stance, but sterner in her appearance.

"He's awake," the older one says, not *to* me of course.

The young one, probably an intern like Jos was, reacts immediately, whipping out her tablet in front of her as if all of the answers are written there – for all I know they probably are. The older woman, I'm guessing my new Doc, watches her minion with a steadily raised eyebrow. It's actually kind of impressive how smug and "in-charge" she contorts her face, as if mastering that look is all that being a Doc requires. My last Doc, Isaacs, certainly never completely mastered that flare; he was smug in his own bubbly kind of way, but Jos was far more "in-charge" than Isaacs ever looked. After everything that happened, Jos trying to sneak me out and using Isaacs as an accomplice, I wonder if either of them will ever step foot in the Freakhouse again, and if they do, which side of the door will they be on?

Damn him. Damn them both! What should I care what happens to either of them!

I clench my eyes, trying to drive them out. I wouldn't be here if it weren't for them! If Jos had just stayed away!

I force my tears back. I think I'm even starting to shake.

If either of the White Coats notice, they don't react much.

The intern scans the barcode on my wrist and then proceeds to check my vitals. She and her supervisor exchange a sort of question and answer period in front of me, but neither of them bother to ask me how I'm feeling. I'm not a patient; I'm a Freak, a broken piece of equipment that they need to repair so that I can be made useful again. I did only just turn twenty years old after all. I'm in my Fresher year with my whole life ahead of me to be experimented upon.

The thought doesn't scare me anymore. A small part of me is still holding onto the idea that Blue will be waiting for me just outside of the door, just like my first clinic day. Ready to catch me.

My tears for him don't burn the same way. These ones aren't fueled by anger. It's something deeper. For some reason it's in my jaw now. I feel it rattling like I'm trying to say something. I'm not though. If I didn't feel my teeth chattering against each other, I probably wouldn't have noticed my involuntary movement at all.

"Clearly the antipsychotic isn't working," Doc says. "He'll need something to make him less restless."

Restless? I've been unconscious for a few days at least! My chattering teeth are clearly telling a different story. Even I can't deny it.

After Blue died I was sedated for days. I was either a pitiful drooling wreck or a spaz throwing a tantrum. Of course the Docs would assume that any attempt at escape would just be a branch of my disturbed behaviour, because why else would anyone ever want to leave such a *happy* place? The Docs lived and breathed the Lantham economic solution – then again, so did everyone on the outside of the Institution, that's why they chose to live in Lantham County. If they didn't agree with the system, they could just leave. I still don't know why my parents didn't. It makes me wonder how things would have played out if Lantham never existed in the first place. Would all of the people I've lost still be with me? Would I have even met *him*?

It's pointless to dream about the *what if's*. This is where I am. I clench my teeth hard. This is my life. This is what's left of it.

I'm digging through what I have left in me. I can feel the bouts of rage that want to burst out, and the pain that I don't dare touch since I just got it locked back up again. Beyond all that, is nothing. There should be something. Anything at all. I know that Blue wasn't the only thing in my world, but I can't even put a face or a name to anything else. It's in there, logically I know it is, but it's so dismissibly small that it might as well be white noise to me.

The intern dutifully scrolls through her options. She recites back something that has at least eight syllables and might even be a small dinosaur. The Doc seems to approve with a beaming tilt of her head.

Great.

The intern processes the request and the Doc has to enter her passcode in order to approve it.

They seem rather satisfied with themselves and continue to gameshow quiz each other as they leave the room. They don't say when they're coming back. I could be re-medicated in an hour or in a week. All I know is that I've been lying in this bed for too long. The straps are starting to piss me off, my mouth is dry, my skin is soggy, I'm parched and starving. I suppose I could have said something while those two White Coats were in the room, but there's not much motivation there when you figure out that they don't even see you as a person. I'm uncomfortable, yes, but anything short of begging isn't likely to do anything. White Coats are generally uncomfortable around us Freaks at the best of times. One might think that we're almost *too* human for them to handle. I'm not in the mood to beg. I'm still hooked up to an IV, so I must be staying alive on that somehow.

I've got nothing to do but lie here. I don't have to sit on my own for long to realize how deafening the silence is to me. It opens me up inside-out, replaying a moment that was anything but silent.

I scrunch up my eyes and shake my head. I can't be in here. I can't be in my own head. I force myself to focus on anything else. Anything that actually exists. I strain to listen to the world taking place just beyond the doors behind me. Other doors are opening and closing. Things are being wheeled around and *clanging*. People pass by having hard-to-hear conversations. At some point a cellphone rings. A few announcements are made, calling specific people to a certain room or to pick up some call on line one-hundred through one-hundred and nine.

It helps. It's useless observations, but it helps. I'm not shaking, my teeth aren't clenched, and my hands aren't even balled up into fists. It's not a cure, though. I'm still fighting with the undeniable reality that I feel like I've been smashed into a thousand pieces. I wish I was still out of it. I wish that I could just close my eyes and roll back to unconsciousness. But I'm too awake now. Too alert, and I know exactly where my idle mind will run to. My body needs to get up and move around. I need to stretch. I need to walk. I need to at least roll over and get off my ass.

With nothing else left to me, I go back to listening. Listening for anything at all.

I hear them coming up the hall before the door even opens. It seems like it's been hours, but who knows with no clock in the room – at least not one I can see or hear.

A couple of White Coats enter. These aren't the same two that checked me over earlier. Their shoes don't even sound the same, and now that I can see them, both wearing medical masks, it's clear that they aren't built the same either. Four dark uniformed attendants join them. Something's about to go down.

A new mask comes in. He's the tallest White Coat in the room; he even looms over the attendants. He looks me over. I can only see his eyes, worn and crow-footed but stern. He's not afraid to look me in the eye. It unnerves me more than I could have ever guessed it would. He just stands there, staring, letting the others bother to scan and check me over. He never takes his eyes off of me.

I want to throw-up. I'm scared now; not of what's going on, but by him. I'm also transfixed and can't look away.

It isn't until one of the White Coats moves in front of my line of sight with a syringe that I even notice what's happening. It's empty; she already used it. Whatever it was is now slowly flowing through me. I feel myself getting heavier. I feel my world getting hazier, and yet those piercing eyes from that sunken face are still staring into me…

I wake suddenly, as if in a panic, but my brain hasn't quite told me why yet. That's when I notice what's so strange. I've jolted up. I'm sitting upright, leaning against my own arms. I'm not restrained. I'm in that same small, overly-clean Doc office. The charger is still there, charging nothing.

I check my body. I'm not plugged into anything. I don't even feel as clammy as I remember feeling the last time I woke up. I still feel all pinched up inside, a few joints and muscles feel out of place, but I also don't feel like I just narrowly survived a five-hundred story drop either.

I do have to pee though. I guess that's what got me up so fast.

I swing my legs over to the side of the bed. They're stiff, but I'm just glad that I can move.

Getting around the safety rails of the patient bed is more challenging than I'd have thought, especially since I ache something terrible, and fancy maneuvering, even just scooting down, is quite an ordeal. I push myself through it and get onto my feet, wobbly in the worst way, but I manage to throw myself against the rail of the bed to lead me to the wall; it's a bit harder from there.

Fortunately it turns out that the jutted out wall was concealing more than a closet. I do have a washroom! It's the closest thing I've come to something pleasant in a long while. As much as I have been determined to keep torturing myself, this was just not a luxury I could withhold from myself.

My relief is short-lived. I'm not finished, but I hear the door open to my room. I hold my breath, and everything else, and stay very quiet. I don't know why; I'm not trying to hide. I'm sure that the door requires me to be scanned in and out, so really, if I'm not on that bed, where else could I possibly be? Maybe I'm afraid that they're just going to strap me back up. Maybe I'm afraid of that new drug they're going to stick me with, if they haven't done so already.

I wait just a little while longer. I don't hear anything else, so no one left the room either. I tell myself to breathe again. I can have this one moment to myself. I can finish what I came in here to do and walk out with my head held high.

I wobble back out. My head isn't sitting as high as I would have liked, but I will accept just having the washroom as victory enough for one day. At least I know that my hands are clean – who knows how long I've been sweating in a bed without being washed.

Leaning against the wall gets tricky as it disappears to bring me to the open room. I study more than the floor beneath me so that I can figure out how to maneuver closer to the bed. I know that I'm not alone in here, but if they weren't panicked enough to break down the door and haul me off of the toilet, then they can wait until I'm ready to acknowledge them.

The bed seems forever away, but I make it. I stand with my back to it, content enough to lean rather than sit. I look over. My heart stops.

So that's what I'm afraid of. Thank goodness I just emptied my bladder because I'm positive that if I hadn't I would have just pissed myself.

"So. Here you are," he says blandly, altogether unimpressed and unsurprised.

The tall lankiness, the sunken skeletal face, the accusing cold eyes, the low dismissive voice. I didn't need to read his badge to know.

"Doctor Parish," I mutter so quietly that I can barely hear myself.

He's leaning against the desk, not quite sitting on it, his hands in his doctor's jacket pockets.

I'm a helpless child again. I vividly remember every intimidating moment I had growing up in Dr. Parish's home – and across from it. I was practically family in the Parish house, at least as far as his wife and son were concerned, but never him. I was nothing but trouble to him. A bad kid from a messed up family. I've always known that Dr. Parish worked in the Institution, but none of my friends, my roommates in my ward, had ever mentioned him. He didn't deal with kids. His research was serious – at least it was more than five years ago from what Jos had ever told me. Parish was one of the most acclaimed and respected researchers in Lantham. Since being brought to the Institution, I had always feared what would wait for me at the hands of the White Coats when my time came, but I never considered I'd be at the hands of Dr. Tom Parish.

I'm done for.

"Have a seat," he says, completely monotone.

I don't move. Not only do I not want to move in closer towards him, but the thought of even going near that bed again makes me sweat.

He just stares at me. I don't know if he thinks I'm being defiant or am just completely stupid. He clearly doesn't have patience for me either way. I bow my head down and back up against the wall.

He lets out an audible sigh.

"Have it your way," he says, abandoning the desk and rolling out the chair from behind it. He sits down facing me, his legs crossed.

"You've caused a great deal of grief around here," he says.

What an appropriate word. I wonder if he even recognizes how fitting it is or if he just naturally condescends everyone. Neither would surprise me much.

I don't look up at him. Maybe I hope that he'll not recognize me, or forget about who I was; not that I think he'll go any easier on me.

"Are you deliberately ignoring me?"

I shake my head. "I'm not ignoring you," I say meekly. "I hear you."

"Sit," he commands.

I don't know why, but my response is automatic. I've already sat on the edge of the bed. I still won't look at him though. I can't.

"I want you to know that this is out of my hands," he says.

I look up. Was that a hint of emotion?

"I don't know exactly what my son promised you," he continued, "but I can guess well enough."

"He meant well," I say, unexpectedly even to myself.

"I'm sure he thought he did. He's a wanted man now. He will never have any hope for a future here."

"They bringing him in?" I ask.

"No. He's already across the border."

"So he's okay, then."

"That's one way of looking at it."

A silence permeates between us for a while.

"Dotan," he begins.

I feel my blood drain. Of course he'd know my name; he has all my records in my barcode. He's also the first White Coat to use my name – first *real* White Coat. Jos was never really one of them. Parish of all people would be the last person I'd expect to call me by name. I don't remember him ever doing so before I was a Freak.

"There's a cost to everything," he continues. "You understand that you cannot be allowed to re-enter the Beta Ward?"

Beta Ward? I have no idea what that is.

It takes less than a minute, but eventually I figure it out. He means that I can't go home – the only home I have – D46. The last five years of my life were spent in that room.

I squeeze my eyes shut. I had said my goodbyes, but I guess I figured that if I was going, I'd be out on the other side, not still trapped in here. Froggy, Bear, Marlene, and the Skid. I can't imagine being in a different room. It's been hard enough being in D46 without Blue; so hard that I couldn't sleep in my own bed without him so I had to claim his. Being on the top bunk was the last connection I had to him. If I can't go back to D46, where will I ever find Blue again?

A burning tear streams down my face. I rub it away harshly. I won't do this in front of Parish. He'd never understand.

"You've made it further than anyone in the history of your ward has before. We can't let you go back. Even without an accomplice, it's too great a risk."

"You think I'd do it again?"

"I'd think that only if you had actually left. I've seen the footage. You could have made it."

"But I didn't."

"No, you didn't. But you could have," he says. "Why *did* you turn back?"

I get up and pace back towards the wall.

"It doesn't matter," I tell him sharply.

"You had a rare opportunity. It didn't interest you? Your freedom?"

I choke out a weak grunt of a laugh. "*Freedom?* It doesn't exist out there anymore than it does in here. At least in here you don't pretend like it does."

I don't believe it; Parish almost smiles.

"You actually prefer it in the ward?" he asks me, disbelief and curiosity thick in his voice.

"It's not the ward," I confess.

He doesn't press more from me. I have to give him credit for that.

"I can't promise that you'll find that same resiliency in your new placement," he says.

We hold the stare for a short while. I don't know the other wards. I know that Skids come out of one, and Freaks who age-out go into a different one. I don't fit either of those categories. I have no idea where they want to put me.

"Why tell me? Why not just drop me in head first?" I ask.

"My only son is a fugitive. I think I have the right to try to understand why."

I'll let him blame me. Jos has enough to worry about. Whatever his father thinks of him won't hurt him much now, and whatever his father thinks of me won't save me.

"And why you didn't go with him," he adds. "You won't fight me on this, will you?"

I shake my head. There's no point.

"I don't want to make this messier than it already is," Parish says. "The attendants will escort you, but you'll be in my care from this point on, as you were originally meant to be."

What?

He must have read my face.

"Believe me, it was no accident that you and my son ended up paired. Josiah took the liberty of abusing several passcodes, including mine. I've spent a good long while undoing his changes. I've set it right now. You'll be treated accordingly, I assure you."

Jos overrode the system? I knew that he was manipulating Isaacs, but I had no idea that he had changed my whole profile. So I was supposed to be Parish's all along. No wonder Jos was trying to save me. My heart leaps into my throat. Maybe I should have left with him.

3

BACK TO SKID

As promised, Parish calls in the attendants to take me out. I go willingly enough. Maybe I'm tired, maybe I just know that it's pointless. The fight in me has fizzled out. I'm in that empty space again. I'm here, I'm seeing, I'm hearing, I'm processing it at some level, but it still doesn't mean anything. It doesn't sink in. Or rather, it feels like there's nowhere for any of this to sink to. I'm not going to D46. That at least should mean something. I know it should. But it doesn't. Or maybe I've just already accepted it. Everything I knew, everything I was, it's all over now.

I have to be re-processed. I remembered this all too well. My picture taken. My head shaven. My picture taken again. Thankfully I am already branded so I don't have to go through that again. Both wrists, both calves, and the back of my neck. I feel naked again, like a Skid. Seems appropriate enough.

I have no idea where I am in the building. I'm led down ramps, into a service elevator with no floor buttons, and I have no idea how many floors we've passed. All I know is that we're heading down. My old ward was up. I remember that first elevator ride. If there was any doubt about which floor I used

14

to live on, just getting on top of that rooftop like Blue and I used to do was proof enough that we were pretty high up.

No. There it is again. I suck in too much air and hold it in as long as I can. *Not now.* I just want the nothing. *I'm sorry.* Just for this. *I just can't.* Just to help me get through whatever's waiting for me.

I decide to focus on the mundane. It worked before, I can do it again. I listen to the hum of the florescent lights above me. The reeling of the elevator down the shoot, which isn't nearly as rickety as I need it to be at this moment. I would have loved the grinding of metal on metal, some audible *clicks* every time we pass a floor. I wouldn't call this elevator silent, but for this one time in my life I want it to truly feel like the animal cage it is. I am the feral animal, aren't I? I even wish that I could live up to that idea. I'd bare my teeth and tear down everything in front of me.

I think everyone in this metal box feels the disappointment. I take a second to look at the two goons at my side. Their black uniforms perfectly pressed, even their berets tilted at the same angles. And while neither of the men look anything alike, they've practiced their stone cold stare so perfectly that they might as well be clones.

At least my escorts are providing me the dark atmosphere I'm otherwise lacking. Though I'm sure that there's nothing pretty waiting for me once these door open. Considering that I just came from a windowless room, and am now standing in a windowless box, I'm sure that going straight down isn't a good sign of what's to come. I'll probably never see sunlight again. I imagine a dank dungeon where they shackle up all of the bad seeds, hang us up to rot. Maybe Parish's Frankenstein lab is down here, ready to mash together our broken bodies to make some real Freaks.

I breathe out. I'm as ready as I'll ever be.

The elevator opens and the hallway we enter is just as nondescript as any of our common areas: bland metallic walls that seem to curve instead of conforming to straight lines, no windows, just yellow-tinged florescent lights, except that these ones seem to flicker far worse than any I've seen, even in the laundry room.

The attendants don't speak to me, they just walk me down. We stop in front of a door. They don't move. It's eerie how solider-like they are, no feeling, no slouching, they don't even blink, or at least it seems that way. I do my best to copy them. I hope that it at least looks like it's working.

I see the scanner. They've stopped a clear distance from it. I know the drill. They've brought me as far as they need to, and I'm not putting up a fight. Out of habit, I raise my wrist to the scanner. It reads me, but I don't get a warm automated welcome like I did five years ago. The screen flashes up my picture and details. It's approved me.

The doors open and I walk into a transition room. I scan myself again after the door behind me closes. The same image pops up on the screen, me, but this time a number shows up beside me. 0-17. There's no map, no guide, but again it's approved me, and the door in front of me opens. I have no idea where I'm going, but there's no turning back.

Once the door fully opens, I realize why I won't be needing a map. I'm in a room full of rooms – cells more like. I've never been in a prison before, but I can imagine that this is not too far off. It's like a library with rows of shelving, only in this case it is pillars of cement block walls framing steel bars. I'm not counting exactly, but from where I'm standing, I can see at least five blocks of "shelves" on each side of me. Staring dead ahead, I can barely make out how far down it is to the next wall. The pillar-like wall in front of me has two numbers painted in white, each one with an arrow pointing outwards.

← 180 195 →

If this is directions, I've got a long walk ahead of me. I go left, all the way to the end, reading the painted numbers as I go. I can see the wall at the end; I'm nearly at it.

← 30

I look across the way. I'm at the very start of the line. Somewhere down here I'm bound to find my place. I make my way down. The bars go all the way down. If it weren't for sheets tied up to the sides, I wouldn't know from looking where one cell ends and the other begins. It's unsettling seeing all of these clearly lived-in spaces and not seeing a single soul around. It's like an overnight ghost town, but in a dark underground prison warehouse.

There it is, 17. The steel-bar door is wide open. It's bare. A metal frame, a worn thin mattress, a small sink and a toilet in the back corner. With open bars as walls, there's no privacy on three sides of me, and I guess not much from across the way either. No dresser, no table, no chair. I don't even see a pillow or a bedsheet. I haven't walked into the cell yet. I'm by myself, what possible motivation do I have for going in? It's empty. It's so empty…

I turn out, keeping my blurry eyes on the cement floor. I can feel my teeth clench again, my knuckles straining to maintain a fist. The cell has slapped me in the same way that seeing Blue's empty bed did. I can't live in the echo of that. I can't –

I swallow hard. I flex my right hand. What I wouldn't give to have him grab it now. He would, too. He'd jump out as if from nowhere, grab my hand and lead me running down to who-knows-where. He'd see this whole thing as an adventure. A new jungle gym to climb around on.

At least until nightfall.

No. Not yet.

I make a fist and let that dig its way into my stomach. I turn around.

Chills go through me as I enter and get a view from the inside. I guess this was more how I used to imagine the Lantham Institution to be when we used to study it in school. *"Only orphans and criminals get sent there."* I guess I fit both categories now. Congratulations, Dr. Lantham, your genius economic solution has proven itself invaluable. Here I am, twenty years old with nothing to live for. You win. I'm yours. I give up.

I toss myself down on the mattress. I can feel the springs poking through. The metal bedframe squeaks and scratches against the cement floor. Despite my new confined quarters, this feels too open. There's at least twelve feet of empty space above me. In the dim light I can barely even see the outline of all of the bars that complete this cage. I'm going to have a hell of a time trying to sleep like this.

I lift up my hands and bend my palms back, trying to remember how close Blue's bunk was to mine. I'd give anything to have Blue let his hand drop down from that top bunk just once more.

Running my fingers through thin air just isn't the same.

I turn myself over, facing where Froggy and Bear's bunk should be. All I see is toilet.

I sit up.

The cells around me have put up sheets, tied to the bars between us, providing a small bit of privacy. I hope that I get a set of supplies soon. I have nothing else to wear, nothing to sleep on, and no real idea where, or if, I'll find a shower. Maybe they do expect me to sponge bathe with that tiny sink, but you'd think that they could at least provide the sponge.

I glance around. I don't even get toilet paper.

This is so pathetic. Me. I am. I've lost Blue. D46. Bear. Froggy. Marlene's all on her own. And I still have the nerve to worry about how I'm going to wipe my butt from now on?

I bury my face in my hands. I'm losing it. I feel like I've got nothing holding me together.

How am I going to do this?

I almost cry. A part of me actually wants to now. I don't know why I don't, why it isn't coming out. I guess I've just got nothing left in me. I'm hungry, I'm thirsty, I'm alone, and it's my own damn fault.

I force myself up to my feet. I go to the sink and turn the tap. It makes a rumbling sound before spewing anything out. It comes out white in a haphazard spray. It's as good as it's going to get, I figure. I cup my hands and drink from it. It doesn't taste any different than what I've grown used to in my old ward. I guess I was half expecting it to be brown and partially containing sewage. I don't know if I should feel relief in that they aren't trying to kill me right away.

Suddenly my whole body vibrates and my heart nearly pops out of my mouth! Without warning every cell door spontaneously slams open. It scares me half to death. Mine is still open, so nothing's changed about that, but I peek my head out to see what's going on.

Sure enough, *every* door is open. My guess is that these inmates are coming back. It's only now that I realize how strange it is that I didn't have to scan myself into my own designated cell, that right now I could walk into any one of these other rooms and it doesn't look like any scanner would stop me.

I don't have any real desire to go walking into these strangers' cells; what scares me is that they can probably just as easily walk right into mine. I don't know anything about these people, but I can imagine that if this is where they've been placed, I'm probably fresh meat to them.

I'm feeling extremely vulnerable right now. I saw how many rows are out there. There's well over three hundred cells if each row is like this one, and if each cell is occupied. I do not want to be readily out in the open when they start coming in. *Maybe they don't know about me yet. Maybe they won't even notice that a new guy is in here.* I don't even believe myself, but it was worth trying. I hear a familiar beeping and the sliding of a scanner-controlled door, several of them.

They're coming!

I rush to the cell door to see if I can move it. I can. I close it, but there's no way to latch it. It must be automatic. I leave it closed and run back to the uncomfortable mattress. I hope I'm not noticed.

The place instantly gets louder. Boisterous voices are bouncing off of the walls, paralyzing me. They're closer than I thought. Their doors must be along the wall closest to me, opposite from where I came in. That's not comforting.

Sure enough I see bodies pass by. I try to control my heavy breathing. They walk lethargically by, wearing grey and off-white simple cotton clothes, even more simple than what I've been wearing for the past five years. Not one of them has looked my way yet. So far so good. They seem just as tired as we did after a day of tasks in D46, but I guess there won't be any running to the showers. I haven't seen a shower down here yet.

"Well, well, well," I hear. I look around, but I don't see anyone in that corridor even looking at me . "New blood," the voice says with a sort of dry cackle that he chokes on.

It's coming from the next cell. He's behind the sheet on my left side. I can see him now; he's pulled a corner back. He's old. He has a small head with tight skin around his cheeks but loose at the corners of his mouth. As he laughs, I see that he's missing teeth – all of them.

"Well lookie here."

I jump as a new voice speaks out from behind me. This makes the toothless guy behind the sheet cackle again – and then spit audibly.

"Where'd you come from, boy?" the guy in the cell on my right asks. He, too has pulled the makeshift curtain over.

So much for privacy.

This guy's older too, maybe not as old as Toothless, at least he doesn't look as worn. His skin is darker with thinner wrinkles on his forehead. He doesn't smile with an open mouth, but the way his jaw sits it seems like he probably has more to him than Toothless. His voice is deeper, slower, calmer.

I'm in no mood for conversation. I don't even try to reply.

Toothless cackles again. "Cat got your tongue?"

"You got yourself a name, boy?" Deepvoice chimes in.

"Sure," I mutter.

Toothless cracks up again. A sort of whistling sound sends chills up my spine and I already know that I hate these people. "Sure is a funny name," Toothless croaks.

"You scared, boy?" Deepvoice asks as if we're letting each other in on a secret.

I just glare at him. I don't know if he's going to try to scare me, tell me horror stories about life on the inside. Little does he know that I'm no Skid. He can't scare me. I won't let him.

Deepvoice cracks a smile, the whole while Toothless is just making noise.

"No, you ain't scared," Deepvoice says. "You must sure be a tough nut, not worryin' 'bout what's gonna happen to ya. I sure can respect that, yes sir. But it don't do no good pretendin' you thick, boy. You in for a long slow ride, yes sir."

"Real slow," Toothless chimes in.

"You'll come 'round. Maybe not today, maybe not tomorrow, but you see, you see real soon. Soon you's gonna get hungry, you's gonna get cold, and you gonna realize that life gets that much harder, that much more miserable. You be talkin' then, yes sir, you be talkin'."

"It's a lonely place," Toothless says. I don't like the grin on his face as he says it.

A loud buzzer sounds. I jump up. There are no screens, not that I can see. There's not even an announcement.

"Closin' time," Toothless says.

"Warnin' bell," Deepvoice adds.

"Warning for what?" I ask. I wish I had a screen to consult instead.

"Bedtime," Deepvoice says as though it explains everything.

I notice that their cell doors are still open.

"They lock the doors?" I ask, pretty sure that I already know the answer.

"Yes, sir," Deepvoice says. "All men to bed who's goin' to bed." He almost lets himself laugh a little. I prefer his belly laugh to the high-pitched whistling and back-of-the-throat croaking of the guy across from him.

"Why not stay out?" I ask. I'd rather sleep in the Rec hall than know I was going to be locked in at night.

"Maybe you don't like to sleep comfy, but at my age, boy, my bed's the best place in this here whole wide world. You feel free to take the floor if ya wants to."

The buzzer goes off again. Just as it stops, the barred doors all snap shut. I had already closed mine so it didn't look nearly as dramatic when the latch locked itself in place.

This is it. I officially have nowhere else to go.

"That's it, then," I say to myself mostly.

"Yes, sir. You expectin' somethin'?" Deepvoice asks me.

"No. Nothing," I say, and scoot myself further down on the bare mattress.

"Doors open at six, boy," Deepvoice tells me as he starts taking down the sheet separating us. "I suggest gettin' in a good sleep before then."

He lumps the sheet and tosses it to me through the bars between us.

"Ain't much of a welcome present, but then again, it ain't much to be welcomed to."

I lean over and pick it up.

"You don't need to welcome me. I've always been here," I say and show him my wrist. 001014126.

"No kiddin'?" He genuinely seems to be in disbelief. "How old are you, boy?"

"It's my Fresher year," I tell him.

"Your what-now?"

"I'm twenty. I'm fresh on the chopping block," I explain.

He does something that's kind of a laugh and kind of a sigh at the same time. "And you got a name for that?"

"It's not my name," I say.

"So you's from the inside, huh?"

I don't say anything.

"What in the hell'd you do, boy? You kill somebody?" the pitch in his voice and the stream of laughter that he's currently engaged in tell me that he doesn't expect a word of it to be true; but how can I deny it? Blue would still be alive if it weren't for me. Yeah, I killed somebody.

I don't tell him any of that, but he must have guessed at least some of it because he stops laughing.

"Don't normally get kids like you down here in Zero Block."

"Zero Block?"

He just smiles.

"Ground Zero, some call it. We's the first. The original *solution*," he says, a slight laugh in his voice. "You in the heart of history, boy. You from the County, then, huh?"

"I was. It's been a long while," I say.

"Ain't much of your kind down here. You in with the imports, boy."

"Imports?"

"Ah, yes sir. That old doctor man says he gots a solution, a place to put what no one wants far out of reach. Lord if that don't sound so sugar-sweet to where they've got more trouble than what they know what's to do with. Zero Block help lighten the load, so to speak. I ain't never seen no Lantham before this here place."

His story catches me off-guard. I just met this guy. He has no reason to tell me anything, in fact, I kind of wish that he wouldn't. It's hard to hate people who humanize themselves in front of you.

"And ol' Joe, there, he's much the same, but came much after me, y'understand."

"So you come here when you've already been in a jail," I say, not really asking, just restating.

"Seems so. That's why a young boy like you bein' here is so curious-like. Thought they had a special place for boys."

"They've got a few," I reply.

"And you go and get yourself kicked down here? Mercy you *is* a tough nut!" He smiles in good humour. "You gonna be alright with just that ol' thing?"

I look at the crumpled sheet in my hand.

"Better than what I had. Thanks," I say sincerely. "Six you say?"

"Yes sir."

"Then what?"

"You gets an hour, just one hour, then you work. Then you gets another hour. Then you sleep. Every day."

"So when can I get my stuff?" I ask.

"*Your stuff*? What *stuff* you got?"

"Clothes and stuff."

He laughs.

"Mercy, boy. D'they hand you goody-bags upstairs, boy? Ain't no goody-bags in Zero Block. You need somethin', you better hope you's a hard worker, boy."

I spread the sheet out. Thankfully it's long enough to reach my toes. The lights haven't gotten any darker, but already I can hear the snores echoing all around, and none louder than that aggravating back-of-the-throat whistle gurgling out of the guy beside me. At least I'll be distracted enough by my surroundings that I probably won't be thinking about the pains in my stomach all night.

"They feed you, boy?"

The way he reads my mind startles me. I shake my head.

"When you last eat?"

I shrug. I have no idea the last time I was actually given solid food. It must have been breakfast before the escape.

"You'll learn quick that you can't last long without food in your pocket and water in your hand." He digs into his pocket. It looks like oatcake. He tosses it through the bars. I take a hungry bite, but I savour the chew. "Bein' sore and sullen won't win you friends on this side, boy. We's more helpful than we look."

"I didn't come here for friends," I mutter.

"Ain't nobody chooses to come here, no sir. But you's here, and you's stuck here until the good Lord calls you up. Like I said, boy, at my age, you need some comfort. Down here, you age fast, boy. Don't deny no comfort. Never know how long you'll be keepin' it."

"Thank you." It's all I can think of to say to him.

"Abe," he says.

It feels weird to be given an actual name. I don't know if I can bring myself to use it. I also realize that he's expecting some form of exchange. A name for a name. All I can think of is D46. It may not be my room anymore, but it's still who I am.

I take another bite and avoid the exchange altogether.

"Sleep well, boy," he says, giving up on me I suspect. I

certainly would.

I take one last bite and put the rest on the edge of the bedframe. The coarse texture of the oats scratch my throat and having just that little bit in my stomach makes my insides feel weighed down uncomfortably.

I'm not sleepy, but I feel done. I curl myself up in that sheet, pulling it up over my face. I use my arm as a pillow and put my other arm over my ear to try to drown out the sounds around me. It doesn't help much, and squishing my own head isn't very comfortable. Nothing about where I am right now is comfortable, I don't care what Deepvoice says.

I scrunch my eyes tight. *I deserve this*, I tell myself. I think back to finding Blue in that stairwell – how bent his limbs were, how much blood pooled from under him, how violently his body spasmed. It plays out horrifically in front of me, stuck on repeat. It hurts to cry but it's the only thing I can bring myself to do.

I'm right here, I tell him. *I'm still here.*

4

DAY ONE

The doors crash open, causing me to jolt, falling off of the bed. *Still here.*

I don't know how I managed it, but the oatcake is still sitting up on the frame. I think about eating more, but I have no idea what's ahead of me, and I have the feeling that the social cafeteria I'm used to won't be found here.

I untangle my legs from the sheet and go to the sink. I rinse out my mouth and then swallow a gulp.

"Mornin', sunshine," Toothless whistles to me. I shudder.

He's at my open door, staring at me.

I had thought about using that toilet, but I can't bring myself to do it now. I question if I even have anything to let out anyways.

I grab the oatcake and stuff it in my pocket. I'm sure that it won't actually fix the pain in my stomach or the heaviness I feel in my head, but I don't know what the food situation is going to be like.

"Don't think he cares much for me," Toothless says amusedly, talking to Deepvoice behind my back. He's right, I don't.

"Warned that boy about bein' sore. He'll learn someday,"

Deepvoice says. "Come along, then."

I follow Deepvoice's lead, not because I really want to be under anyone's wing right now, but I feel like trying to set out on my own would be a really stupid move for someone who doesn't even know where the food is.

I look around my empty cell. Shouldn't I be doing something before leaving my cell? Either hiding my only blanket or locking up the door? What's going to stop someone from just taking it if I leave? It's one thing if it were mine, but I'm pretty sure that blanket is just on loan. I don't care much for owing a debt. Sure we did favours for each other all of the time back in D46, but we were family. I won't be bound to these people any more than I have to be. Right now, I just need something worthwhile to fill my stomach.

I close the cell door but I can't control the latch.

"It'll be fine," Deepvoice says, once again reading my thoughts.

I never actually walked along the back wall. I'm awestruck by how many doors there are on this side. There looks to be a door for each four rows, at least that's the best I can describe it; there's an unbelievably large number of people packing into these doors. I mean, we used to gather all of the time in the cafeteria, even the rec hall, but things were always staggered, made it seem more controlled. Not to mention more cleanly. I feel like I'm surrounded by pirates – the scurvy kind. All I see are heavy brows, faded tattoos, and sweat stains that are probably twenty years old drenched into their sleeveless shirts. If I had a wallet, I'd be checking for it every five seconds in this madhouse.

Eventually I have no choice but to be swallowed up inside of the pool of sweat as we squeeze ourselves through the double-wide doors. It doesn't occur to me until I'm over the threshold that there is no real barrier. No transition room to force us into an orderly line. No scanning. No alarms. No monotone computer voice giving orders. The things you never think you'd actually miss. And I don't, not really. I mean, at the end of the day it's still just another form of herding human cattle around, but it was familiar at least. Another bit of white noise that you don't notice until it isn't there anymore.

I can't help but wonder what the guys would be doing right now. Given that it's somewhere around six in the morning – though how Deepvoice knows that is beyond me, there is no time-telling device anywhere that I can see so far – I bet they're still sleeping.

It's easy to picture the one set of bunks. Bear and Froggy, stacked in the corner by the door. I know that's not how it is now. I know that Bear moved for me right before I left. But I just can't picture it any other way. How could I? I don't want to see Blue's empty bed. I don't want to see someone else lying in it. Right now I can't even picture the way that it used to be. The reality of my current location doesn't allow me to even pretend that things are different; that they could have been different. If I'm down here, it means that Blue isn't anywhere at all.

I clench my teeth and push the thought out. It'll never go away, I know that, but if I let it linger with me too long, I'll probably shatter from the inside out, hollowed out, empty. Who am I kidding? That part's already been done. How I'm still walking now? Following the crowd? Must be autopilot.

Despite the crowds, everyone moves briskly. They have purpose in their eyes, and they look ready to plough over anyone dawdling in front of them.

I know that Deepvoice said that we only had one hour to get going. I wonder if these doors will lock behind us for the day. And what happens if you don't get out of bed in the morning? Do they just let you stay locked up in your cell or does an alarm put the building into lockdown like the Freakhouse did?

That's interesting: I can't even make myself think that I'm in the Freakhouse anymore. These aren't Freaks; these are prisoners. Sure a lot of them look off. The flabby guy standing uncomfortably close to my right has weird facial growths that look like his pores were blowing bubbles that never popped. A scrawny guy beside him has sporadic patches of baldness like missing puzzle pieces on his head. And directly in front of me is a guy with a thin beard who keeps twitching and beating his head down against his shoulder in no patterned rhythm. You'd think this would somehow feel familiar to me, but I can't wrap my head around it being the same. Up top, at least we seemed like we could have had our whole lives ahead of us. This bunch, well, I might have to periodically remind myself that they're human. Maybe it's because they're the most adult people I've been around who weren't wearing uniforms. They should be clean, stern, and doing the herding, not trapped in an oversized ant-farm.

I follow Deepvoice and Toothless through to one massive room. There's nothing in it, nothing that I can see anyway. There's no order to anything in the giant hall. Hundreds, if not thousands, of people are milling about. I can barely make out what's ahead of me due to the swarms around me. But on we go, pushing our way through. It isn't until I can see the doorframe up ahead that I realize that this *is* the transition room.

"You cook, kid?" Toothless asks me.

Ha. Cook? Me? As if they'd even let us use a toaster!

"I'd figure it out if I were you," Deepvoice warns me. "Any ol' idiot can scrub a pot or two, but ain't nobody gonna let good food go to waste. You want to earn some respect 'round here, you gotta contribute. Life gets hard for the man who only serves hisself."

I feel the oatcake in my pocket. All this talk of food is making my stomach cramp up again. What I wouldn't give to be back in the caf, filling up a tray without a second thought about when I'd get to eat again. Since when did I consider the Freakhouse to have luxuries?

"You want to eat," Deepvoice continued, "you gotta give. We run the greenhouses, the farms, the livestock. The Gatekeepers, they take their quota, that's how boys like you get fed every day, but the rest is ours. Work hard, bring it in, and you'll do just fine."

I guess I never really thought about where our food came

from. I mean, we had greenhouses of our own, but I think that was more like garden therapy than actually harvesting.

We come to an old fashioned type of kitchen, one of those big ones you see in movies where a hundred servants roast a whole animal in a giant fireplace. There's no roast, but the activity around each surface is much the same. Several stove tops are manned with pots boiling, and in the walls are ovens. A huge metal door is off to the side and an assembly line of prisoners are passing out bread, eggs, and sacks of oats or flour. So it isn't chaos. These people are like ants, each going in his own way, overlapping one another, but somehow all still so purposeful in their own specific task.

Deepvoice leads me closer.

"You want to eat good, you make a friend fast, boy."

At a row of high-sitting counter space, a huge grizzly man with an eye patch is kneading dough. Something about this pirate elbow-deep in flour is more menacing than if he had me at knife point. Must be because I'm still waiting for the knife to come out.

"Mornin' Laz," Deepvoice says, almost as if he's bowing down to this rough beast.

The Beast just grunts. I can't tell with his one visible eye if he's glaring downwards or just concentrating on what he's doing. Either way I'm just glad that he isn't staring me down. I'll probably live longer if he doesn't notice me.

"Got a dishboy here for ya," Deepvoice says proudly.

Shutup! I'm ready to dive under the table. I won't. I can't convince my legs to move that quickly.

The Beast looks up, still glaring, or maybe that eye just doesn't open all the way. He doesn't stop kneading.

It's too late to dive away now anyways.

"Got dishboys," the Beast snarls.

Deepvoice pats my shoulder. "New blood," he says, as if that somehow changes things. "They ain't fed him none."

"Ain't no freebees in Hell," the Beast spits.

"Boy's gotta get in somewhere," Deepvoice adds.

"You gonna let 'im have your share, old man?"

"I get by," Deepvoice said, a lighthearted belly laugh rising up from within him.

Wait? What? He already gave me his blanket! Can't the guy just mind his own business already!

The Beast grunts.

"I'll show 'im the ropes, no problem, he heh," Toothless chimes in with a whistle.

Great. I should have just walked in on my own.

Another grunt.

Toothless grins and takes me by my shirt sleeve. He's stronger than he looks.

"Abe and me, we does the clean-up for ol' Laz. Keeps us in the peckin' order," Toothless says cheerily. "Cooks get best rations, and their workers, we get our names in. Laz always makin' a somethin'. Good man to know!"

Toothless leads me to an assembly line of basins.

"We get limited hot water down here," he explains to me. "We has our own heaters, but still water is worth savin'. Wash by hand, keeps the water.

"We makes our own soap, our own rags – heck, everythin' you see here's been made by these here folks. You bring it in, you gets a share. Pretty simple, ain't it?"

I take a quick bite of my oatcake. I can't believe that I have to impress this lot if I want to eat. Just give me my tray of slop already!

Even I can tell that there's no point in complaining aloud. I have no choice. I follow Toothless's lead.

I've done kitchen duty before, but it always involved putting dishes in the steamer and sorting them. I don't even remember ever needing to hand wash a dish when I lived on the outside. Needless to say, I'm slow at it. It's not just a plate or two coming my way, it's the sticky mixing bowls, forks with so much gunk that you can't even see the prongs anymore, and as I finally get one done, three different people have offloaded an entire basin's worth, one right after the other. I look over at Toothless and all of the other prisoners. They don't take more than a second for every item they pick up. They pass it down the line after the soap station, then it gets rinsed once, twice, and taken up for drying. I'm holding my line up.

"Eggs!" Someone shouts.

"Bread!"

"Cheese!"

Even the words sound good. It's taunting how they shout it out like that.

Deepvoice comes around to us, holding out two cups with spoons. He hands one each to Toothless and me. Toothless savours a bite and then plunges back in.

"I'll take it from here, boy," Deepvoice says.

I gulp down three mouthfuls of the hot porridge before I even start to feel guilty.

"Was this one yours?" I ask him sheepishly.

He laughs from his belly. "Boy, if that one was mine I wouldn't let you so much as sniff it!"

I gulp more down.

"You do your part and, who knows, maybe one day there'll be bacon in it for you."

Toothless cackles and whistles. "How I miss bacon. Be sure you keep yer teeth!" He chomps down, showing me his gums, and then cackles again.

Fortunately I have already cleaned out my cup so the sight doesn't prevent me from being able to eat. Even afterwards I still wouldn't mind some of that bacon they were talking about.

Deepvoice takes my cup and tosses it into the basin. "You ain't done yet," he chuckles at me.

I plunge back in, but compared to the two guys around me, I'm hardly doing half as much work. I'm not trying to be lazy about it or anything. I just don't get into the rhythm I suppose. It also probably means a lot more to them. This has been their way of life forever. Even though I know I'm wrong, I still feel like maybe I'll wake up back at D46 and have things like this done for me. I never thought I'd say this, or even think it, but man we had it easy up there.

The morning already seems never ending, but I guess it

wasn't nearly as long as I had thought. The buzzer rings.

"Just drop it, kid," Toothless calls to me. "It ain't worth it."

We're not finished, but it's clear that everyone is abandoning their posts.

"What's going on?" I ask.

"We move out."

Task I figure, but I have no idea what my task is for the day. Back in the Freakhouse, kitchen duty was a task. In my mind I should already be half done if it's switchover already.

No one says anything more to me. I wouldn't have heard anything even if they did. There's only three large doors that open for us, and the hundreds of us are all trying to get out.

I can't believe my eyes. I have to shield them for a moment as the sunlight blinds me momentarily. It's barely spring, the air hasn't quite shook off the winter bite yet, but it isn't cold either. I haven't walked outside, on real ground, in years. I should probably relish this moment; smell the dirt or roll in the grass. All I can think of is, *I wish Blue could see this.* It isn't the outside world he dreamed of, but it's something. Besides, knowing him, he'd find a way to hop the fence and ditch this place for good.

I look over at the two story wall that keeps us in. I may not like Zero Block, but I still don't miss the outside world. What I do miss is Blue's version of it. Why can't I escape to *that* place?

The Beast hobbles towards us. I didn't notice while he was at the counter, but he's on crutches. Along with only one eye, he only has one leg, taken off just above the knee if I go by where he ties his pant leg off. He really is a pirate – probably has scurvy and everything. Hanging from his wrist he has four bundles.

"Abe," he calls, and tosses a bundle to him. "Joe." Then he glares at me. "The boy earn it?" he snarls.

"Worked till the end," Deepvoice replies.

Really? I mean, I did, but clearly I did a half-assed job compared to everyone else who was working around me.

The Beast tosses the third bundle at me harshly. He doesn't stay for much longer. He disperses with everyone else. I'm glad when he's gone.

"Lunch," Deepvoice tells me, reading my mind just before I even fully formed the thought.

"We're stuck out here?" I ask.

"Doors open when the workin' day is done," he says, almost cheerfully.

"What if we didn't come out?"

Deepvoice chuckles and Toothless whistles.

"That's when *they* get ya," Toothless answers.

"*They?*"

"Monsters don't live under your bed here, boy," Deepvoice says, and then points up. "And I was told that the devil don't wear white. You don't make use of yourself, they make use of you instead."

"Docs," I say mostly to myself.

"So they calls themselves, but there ain't never been no doctor where I'm from who done what these devils do. Be on guard, boy; it ain't a trip you likely want to come back from."

"I've been," I tell them.

"In the upstairs?"

I nod.

"Beggin' your pardon, but I has a feelin' that they's got a whole mess of different ways of handling us in the underground. If it's a hierarchy, we's Zero, and don't you forget that, boy. No, you's still walkin' pretty, so whatever them in white's done to you, it ain't nothing."

I can't argue with him. I want to tell him about some of the horrors I've seen. About Marlene throwing herself to the ground, clawing at her own flesh. About Blue, seizing at the slightest trigger. About perfectly normal people, coming out Freaks. But how can I tell him any of this stuff when the worst I've had it is a little blood-rush? Jos was determined to protect me. Somehow he even managed to pull it off. I'm sure these two have seen some pretty horrible stuff in their time, but I'm not so unfamiliar with it as they may think. I wonder if Deepvoice or Toothless know what it's like to watch someone they actually care about suffer. It's my first day, so I won't compare notes with them, not now.

"What now?" I ask, changing the subject.

"What's your trade, boy?" Deepvoice asks me.

Trade? I remember reading about the Institution in school. That was one of the "benefits" about cleaning out the young people, they'd get an education and a trade. Well, in my five years I wouldn't consider anything they gave me as an education, and as for a trade, I wasn't skilled at anything; laundry duty doesn't build up the skillset very well.

I guess they can read the blank stare on my face.

"You a harvester, a butcher, or a craftsman?" Deepvoice asks.

I shrug. I can imagine that they have no shortages of butchers in this area. The Beast alone probably does it with one hand tied behind his back. And as for the other options, well, the only thing that comes to mind is our own greenhouses. I was never a fan of it, in fact I wasn't much of a fan of any of our task assignments, but it's at least something that I'm familiar with. It was my last task now that I think about it. Blue and I were both assigned to the same task at the same time, something that rarely happened. There was so much on my mind that day, but Blue kept me good and distracted. We ended up having more of a dirt fight than actually being productive. We laughed so hard. I'll never forget that huge grin on his face.

I'm even almost smiling now. *I'm not going anywhere.*

"You alright, boy?"

And just like that I'm back to rock bottom. "I've worked greenhouses," I finally say.

Deepvoice and Toothless exchange looks with one another.

"I'll take the boy," Deepvoice says.

Toothless nods.

At least that puts me with the less creepy of the two.

"I'll be seein' you then… Ain't you got a name boy?" Toothless asks.

"Yeah," I say. I'm not even going to pretend like I'm willing to go any further with this. My roommates were the only people I ever told my name to, and I plan to keep it that way. For everything they confided in me, and me in them, in Blue, it means too much. It's their secret to keep now. The only part of me that'll ever linger back in D46. Just as their names are all I have left of them down here. My secrets to keep. I won't betray them. Not ever again.

"Ol' Joe's a soap man," Deepvoice says to me after Toothless is far behind us and we've begun walking our own direction. This explains why he sounded so proud of it at the kitchens. "I can't get over that work with the animal parts myself, that and the smell. I tip my hat to them, that's for certain. Ain't no easy jobs here."

Deepvoice leads me into the greenhouse. I wasn't prepared for it to be *this* size. The one we used to use could fit maybe a dozen Freaks comfortably, with our attendants and instructors of course. This thing was about the size of the Rec hall, if not bigger. Dozens of prisoners manning rows upon rows of trees, vines, and what looks like indoor sandboxes.

"The big work will take place when the wheat's ready. For now, we just try to keep the produce comin' in nice," Deepvoice said, breathing in the aromas.

It's warm, stuffy, and pretty much smells like manure. I don't remember it being this bad in the small greenhouse.

I realize too late that I should have been asking more questions when I began this task. I can only stand the smell for so long before I feel the little that I have in my stomach churn.

"You turning green there," Deepvoice says with a chuckle. He's elbows deep in the soil. His hands work as if independent from the rest of him. Even as he looks at me, his hands keep on going.

Watching him isn't helping. My head's spinning. I tilt it back, hoping that gravity won't work against me.

"Just outside," he says, trying to reel-in his laughter, "to the left. Can't miss it."

I don't need more permission than that. I bolt out, hardly even registering the directions he gave me. Luckily the part I did take note of, the "can't miss it," was spot on.

I'm confident that this rustic old outhouse and I will become fast friends. I blame the manure, though of course the outhouse doesn't help with that at all. At least that means that I won't be intentionally hiding out in here.

This time I relish in the fresh air as I head back to my task. I close my eyes, and for a moment, I'm on the rooftop.

I have to shake it out of my head. My best memories and my worst one are all attached to the same place. I don't want to dwell on any of them. If I do, they'll all be tainted.

I suck it up and go back inside. Deepvoice is humming to himself. Hardly seems like he even notices when I kneel back down beside him.

"That's for you, boy. Thought you'd need it."

My head's still spinning a little bit, and it doesn't help that I don't know what I'm looking for. My elbow hits it, but thankfully I catch the metal cup before it tips.

There are several metal cups clipped up on chains on some of the pillars. The idea is that you fill your cup with water when you need it, drink it down, and get back to work. I don't know what it says about me that I now have one at my station.

The water tastes like dirt. I try not to refill it too often.

The mugginess is slowing me down. I don't mean to be unproductive. Everyone around me has a rhythm. Despite the long day of labour, the breaks that these guys take are few. I'm still the only one with his own cup, and even though I'm trying really hard to push my endurance, I'm still refilling my water several times between my bathroom runs. At least the water starts to taste better each time.

After a while I notice that even Deepvoice has begun to dig into his bagged lunch. I check around me, though I don't know what I was expecting to see. A clock maybe. Something to tell me when it was lunch time. It doesn't look like anyone is really on break. Deepvoice is munching and working at the same time. Somehow still humming away.

I could use a bite, just to tie me over for another hour. I just pray that it isn't more oatcake. Not that I'm not grateful to have any type of food at my disposal, but I'm sure if I pump much more water for myself someone's going to string me up with the other cups.

I unwrap the cloth bundle that the Beast prepared for me. It has more weight to it than I expected – or maybe it's just my hunger dreaming up what I hope to find.

"Seriously?"

I didn't mean to say it out loud. Sure enough, everyone has stopped moving their hands and is staring at me.

I should just crawl into the dirt now.

"Kid got a problem?" a husky voice bellows out. A big bruiser who looks like he's had a bad day with a bathtub of acid stands up. He pounds an open palm against one of the pillars.

Yup. I should definitely start digging my own grave.

"The boy ain't your business, Jake," Deepvoice calls back sternly. His voice isn't raised, and he's not even looking at the big guy. I don't know if it's his years, but the bruiser makes a sort of growl noise and then turns back around.

I'm not moving a muscle. I don't know if it's safe to.

"You mind telling me what the matter is?" Deepvoice asks me, low enough so that the whole greenhouse doesn't have to hear.

"Nothing," I say. I'm not being defiant. I mean, aside from the obvious issues I've been having, I actually mean 'nothing'.

Deepvoice raises an eyebrow.

I hold up the bagged lunch that started it all. "There's actual food in here."

A bread roll, salted beef, cheese, an apple, and, of course, an oatcake. It's a feast! Even with the oatcake.

His stern face melts away. I see his belly shake all the way up to his shoulders before the laughter erupts from him. He has tears in his eyes, and he lets out a high pitched "ah" as he wipes them away.

He shakes his head as he sets back to his work.

That must mean that I'm in the green. I let myself have a bite of cheese and bread. I can't even put my thoughts into proper order. It tastes like beautiful. I don't want to ruin it by crying, but I can't even promise myself that I won't.

This task never ends. I've watched the sun do a full circuit from one end of the greenhouse to the other. In this time we've gathered a few baskets of tomatoes, beets, and beans. I say *we* very loosely. I was weeding mostly. And refilling water cups. And puking my guts out on more than one occasion. Yes, I'm sure my fellow prisoners feel the benefit of my contribution, especially the Big Bruiser who cracks his knuckles, and sometimes his neck, when we pass by one another. I stay close to Deepvoice. Hell, if Big Bruiser gets any closer, I might be holding Deepvoice's hand all the way back to the safety of my cell.

Just as that thought comes to me, I'm reminded that I can't control the locks on my own door. I'm screwed.

My fingers are stained and raw. Every time a basket gets filled, we set it to the side for pick-up. A parade of prisoners cart away baskets, one after the other, and return for more. I'm told that these guys are responsible for the sorting. They'll take it all to the Staff Centre where it will be processed. When we reach our quotas, the rest will be carted into a storage room. The storage room can be accessed from the inside, it's attached to the huge pantry room.

When I get the chance, I ask Deepvoice about the obvious opportunity just sitting here. "Has anything ever just gone missing one day?"

Deepvoice's forehead wrinkles up as his eyebrows push together.

I continue, "I mean, someone just helping themselves to an early dinner? A few extra helpings?"

His forehead clears and he's nodding now. "It's happened once or twice, to be sure. Some folks can't help themselves. But ain't nobody ever alone here. Ain't nobody doesn't know what you doin'. One man don't leave much trace, but five or six, you notice. It's happened once or twice that some folks think they run the show, that they's more important. Five or six don't matter much when we, the hard workers, show them what's what. Trouble like that don't last long. Here there's always someone to take care of it. We all in it together, boy."

All I want to do is have a hot shower, a bowl of soup, and a bed to sleep in for the next solid week. Deepvoice lets out a deep belly laugh when I tell him.

"Showers are hard to get into, especially hot ones!"

"But there are showers somewhere, aren't there?" Even I know that I'm sounding desperate.

"Oh yes. We have 'em. And we each get a turn," he explains.

"How often do these turns come up?"

He shakes his head, smiling the whole time.

"I get it, I'm pampered," I say.

"Ain't no doubt about that," Deepvoice laughs. "I'm sure we'll find a way to fit you in."

I shudder. I feel extra dirty just thinking about it. I don't like this unmarked routine. I want a schedule. Someone put a timetable up somewhere I can reference. I can appreciate that they don't get too many new arrivals popping up down here, but no one can expect me to just *know* how this all works, how I fit in.

In D Block I showered every day, sometimes even twice a day. I can't believe I thought sharing a bathroom with three guys was rough. I wish I could go back in time and slap myself. I wish I could go back in time and do a lot of things differently.

We all pile back inside, squished up against one another like cattle. Once in, everyone scurries into place. Deepvoice drags me back to the basins. Our unfinished work is sitting there, waiting for us. No shower for me, but I do manage to wash my hands and face really quickly.

Someone's cooking meat. I can smell it. More bread is being baked, probably the stuff that was prepared earlier. I'm starting to realize that whatever is made in our morning hour is rarely what we end up eating in the evening. These guys are always planning ahead. They preserve as much as they can, keep things on rotation, keep people working, and this way they know that they'll all be fed in the next hour, the next day. We never paid that much attention to things in my ward. It was just assumed that we'd always have a meal ready for us – questionable quality perhaps, but always there.

The dishes are never ending. The soap burns my raw fingers in no time. But I don't stop. I just want this day to be done.

"Take a minute while it's hot," Deepvoice says to me, putting a hand on my shoulder to grab my attention.

I almost don't want to give up my momentum. I feel like if I stop I'm just going to fall over. But I do it. I stop. I pull my hands out of the grimy water. It hurts to stretch my fingers out. I reach out for the large cup Deepvoice has brought me and I can see just how badly my hands are shaking.

The cup is scorching. I don't know how Deepvoice managed to carry it all this way for me. I lift up the bottom of my shirt and use it to put at least some distance between me and the metal cup. It's a soup, a thick one with huge chunks of vegetables. After being trapped in a greenhouse all day, I can't help but wonder if I contributed to anything inside this cup. I raise it to my lips, but the steam is making my eyes water. I can feel the heat against my lips without even touching the rim. I can't eat this now.

I look over and see Toothless digging two fingers into his cup, shoveling bits of potato into his gummy mouth. He makes loud stuttering slurping sounds, as if taking a number of breaths in quick enough succession will save his tongue from blistering. Maybe it works. He doesn't even wince. He only pauses long enough to mash away on whatever he can't swallow whole. I should really stop watching people as they eat. It doesn't help me at all.

I raise the cup up again. The steam is still getting to me. I can't risk that first sip. If I get burned, I know I'll jolt and spill the lot of it. For as hungry as I am, I don't want to lose an ounce of food. Just smelling it is going to have to do for now. I set it down at my feet, close by but hopefully I won't accidentally kick it over.

I plunge back into the basin and take up where I left off. I know there's hardly any time left, and I know that the dishes will never end, even with the dozen of us taking it on. It's just easier. It's easier to just push through it. I pick up the rhythm of it again, drown out everything else, and just keep going.

The buzzer rings. A bunch of people just drop whatever they're doing. I've got a two prong fork in my hand. I finish it up quickly and toss it in the next basin. Mine's empty. I hoist it up, going against the flow of prisoners, and take out the soapy muck. I spill enough to soak my right leg, but once I get far enough over from the crowd, it's easier to keep it steady. Dumping it out now will save time in the morning.

The kitchen hall has emptied pretty quickly. Only a few are still trying to get the prepared food back into the storage room. I'm ready to fall into my uncomfortable bed now. I run back over to the basins, carrying my empty one. I place it back and bend down to grab my cup.

"Son-of-a-bitch!"

I shove the basin off its stand. I want to burst into tears. I am so freaking tired. I feel so stupid. I'm surrounded by criminals, what part of my brain could even think that leaving a cup of soup unattended would go over well? I know that I don't have much time. The doors will close on me soon and I sure as hell don't want to try to cozy up on the floor in here.

I run out. I run straight through the cellblocks.

Toothless calls out to me.

I've run too far. I've gone right past my room – my cell. I don't even reply. I just turn around and march in, slamming the barred door behind me, though it doesn't shut; it just bounces back open again and swings a little there. I go to my sink and run the water. I wet my face, take a few drinks, and rub the rest of the water in my cupped hands around the back of my neck.

"You alright, boy?" Deepvoice says through his bars beside me.

I guess he heard me grumbling. I didn't even realize that I was making audible noise – aside from the slamming door anyway.

"Fine," I grunt.

I can hear Toothless's whistling throat laugh from behind his sheet-curtain. He's listening in.

"Ya know, what you did today, boy, we's took notice."

"Great," I mumble.

I take off my shirt. With all of the sweat, dirt, and who knows what else, I have no desire to sleep in it tonight. I have one thin sheet. It's the only clean thing I own right now. *Own.* I don't know, do I even *own* that?

"What're you so sour about? Ain't nobody told you to."

"I know," I say coldly. It doesn't matter why I feel like crap. I expect that I'll be getting used to this sooner or later. "Think my shirt will dry for tomorrow?" I ask, trying to get him off of me.

"Wring it out good, might be okay," he answers me after a little hesitation. "You ain't used to a day's work, are ya?"

I don't bother even acknowledging it. I've got the water running again. I put both my shirt and pants in, just to try to make it somewhat clean for tomorrow. I know I'll be freezing tonight though.

"Boy's hungry," a gruff voice says from behind the curtain in front of me. The Beast. "Boy's blind, too."

I wring out the shirt. I really don't want to hear from any more people right now.

"Yeah, *boy's an idiot*, thanks, I got that!" I grumble.

"Ain't no call for bein' rude," Deepvoice says. "Laz is just tryin' to help is all."

"Ingrates don't last long," the Beast says like it's a threat.

And just what should I be grateful for? I don't say it, but I want to. I tie the shirt sleeves to bars to hang dry. I turn back around to deal with my drenched pants, and that's when I see it. On the bed are folded sheets and my cup of soup. I'm stunned.

I turn to Deepvoice. "Did you?"

"Boy needs to start using his head," the Beast says. "But I bet that's how he got down here in the first place."

I take the cup. It's still hot, but the soup isn't steaming anymore. I take one sip. I already feel myself getting calmer.

"Thank you," I say quietly.

I pick up the top sheet. I don't know how many are stacked here, but it's breaking my heart just to see one here. As I pick up the stack, a few of the smaller ones drop out. They aren't sheets. It's two shirts and a pair of pants – simple ones like cotton pyjamas, like what most people around here are wearing. I've got clean, dry clothes for tomorrow, I've got a couple of sheets to wrap myself in and one to bunch up like a pillow.

"Thanks…" *Beast*, but I can't say that, "Laz." It seems so wrong to say his name, but this isn't my world, this isn't my ward. "And you, too…" *Deepvoice*, "Abe."

I pull the pants on. They're a bit big on me, but they'll do. The shirt, too, could fit two of me, but I don't care about how it fits right now. I spread out the sheets and sit on the bed, cup in hand. I'm so tired and can barely bring myself to finish that last bit. All the broth is gone and I just have stubborn pieces of carrot and potato stuck on the bottom. I scoop my fingers in and dig them out. It almost hurts to take that last bite. I swallow, wipe my mouth with my hand, and just drop.

At first I think I'm dreaming. I hear the crash of the metal bars, the screaming and pleading. All that comes to my mind is the garage: the breaking glass, the slamming door, the shouting, the alarms, the car screeching, my bones hitting the pavement, Blue's voice hollering at me – he's in pain, he is in so much pain, and he's crying out for me – they've got him – they've got him and I can't see what they're doing to him! *STOP IT! LEAVE HIM ALONE!*

But it isn't a dream. I can hear it echoing around me but it must be several rows back. They don't even exit out of the doors near me. No one else is saying a word. It's so quiet –

aside from the screaming – that I can hear the accepted scan before the doors even open. Once they've shut, there is instant silence. I realize that my heart is beating unbelievably fast. So that's how they do it. No warning. I wonder who he was. I wonder why they picked him. I've got Parish out for me; I'm sure my turn won't be too far away.

No one talks about it the next morning. The buzzer sounds, everyone piles into the kitchen hall, and work resumes without a second thought. My basin is empty from last night so I don't feel particularly rushed while other dishwashers will be changing out the water in theirs. I see the Beast, Laz, hobbling around on his crutches, Deepvoice carrying his supplies for him. He grunts at me when he sees that I'm standing at his counter.

"Now what are you missing?" he snarles.

"Nothing," I say. "I'm sorry for not noticing yesterday."

"Keep your eye on your work, boy," he says.

"Can I give you a hand?"

He raises an eyebrow at me. "I've *got* two of those."

I'm convinced that I'm always going to feel completely stupid around this guy. I know when I'm not wanted. The Beast dumps out the dough he had sitting over-night and then hands me the bowl. Back to the basins.

Toothless helps me carry the newly filled tub back to our station and then he brings me new soap. There's already a new stack of dirties waiting for us. I can't believe it's only day two. I already feel like I've been here forever.

5

IN THE SWING

NO! BLUE!

I wake in a cold sweat, again. I'm freezing, but that's not the only reason I'm shaking.

I pull the thin blanket up over my shoulders and hug my arms around my chest as tightly as I can.

It's quiet. It's been quiet these past four nights. Hasn't helped my dreams any. But I guess I don't need much help envisioning my worst nightmare – I lived it.

I hate not knowing what time it is. I don't even know if it's worth the effort to try to go back to sleep.

Forcing myself to sleep hasn't been an easy process. It makes me kind of thankful that I'm usually so exhausted at the end of the day that I just pass out onto the bed and don't have to think about anything. At times like these, I have to think, but luckily I found a safe way to keep my thoughts from wandering. Listening to sounds doesn't work for sleep like it does for calming me down. For sleep I need to use a little more brain power to wear me out. I count memories. I count secrets. I count names.

Tonight I start with Bear. *Elijah Dean*, I remind myself. *Elijah Dean. Came in '99. Sixteen years old. Rachel.* That was her

46

name. *Rachel Cross.*

I try to add in as much detail as possible. I don't always begin with Bear, but I always save Blue for last.

"Those dreams easing up on you any?" Deepvoice asks as we harvest green beans.

I can't be hearing him right.

"Sorry?" I say.

"You mumble, boy, and it don't sound pleasant."

"Sorry." I focus really hard on the precision of my bean picking.

"We's all gots our own ghosts, boy."

I keep focused.

"I's guessing these ones you brought down with you."

Just stay out of it, old man.

I don't think I said it out loud, but Deepvoice responds with, "As you wish."

My bucket is already half full, but now seems like a good time to start counting what I pick. *One. Two. Three.*

I haven't said a word to anyone since the greenhouse. Even loading up the buckets I hardly even looked up long enough to see who I was handing my harvest to. Thankfully most of the others don't care either way. Suits me well enough, I'm ready as ever to get through those dishes and back into my cell. If I keep my brain focused all the way through, I know I'll be out cold by the time I hit my bed.

I'm just about to veer away from the herd and towards my basin when I feel a firm clasp on my left shoulder.

"We're off today," Deepvoice tells me calmly.

"Off from what?"

It doesn't make sense. But he guides me with that hand on my shoulder. Sure enough I see that Toothless and the Beast are up ahead following a different herd out of the kitchen. We're turning down a thin hall I've never had a chance to get a good look at before – probably has something to do with being sandwiched in the middle of a sea of bodies whenever it's time to move.

I can hardly believe it. I hear it first. Then I can taste the humidity. The showers! I was starting to think that they didn't even exist. It seems like it's been forever since I last felt clean.

Ideally I'd like a bit more privacy, but I don't know how long I have so nothing's stopping me from jumping right under the nearest overhead faucet.

Clearly I'm not the only one who feels euphoria in finding a shower. A bunch of guys don't even strip down until they are well under the water, cleaning cloth and skin in the same go.

The water is barely lukewarm, but at least it's wet. I soak up as much time under the faucet as I can. It isn't easy with four other guys around me trying to do the same.

It's a narrow room made even narrower with sixteen of us crowding around four faucets.

Two of the guys standing with me are in and out in a couple of minutes; I guess they have things to do, or no one to grab their dinner for them. I just want to soak this in for the rest of the night, I don't care who's pressed against me.

My heavenly escape doesn't last forever.

A sharp whistle pierces through the thick echo of running water, followed by "Boy!"

The Beast is calling the shots and I have to follow. Well, I guess I don't *have to*, but he is the source of my dinner, so I'm willing to do whatever he says.

Toothless is holding up our faithful leader as he dries off and dresses. Deepvoice hands me a small thin towel that can barely absorb anything. I use it anyway.

My clothes are soaking wet, and clean, so I don't even bother trying to put them back on. I wrap that towel around me and feel good to go. I wring out my clothes as best as I can and find my shoes in the pile by the door. I slip my feet in, they stick and squish, and I know even just walking a short distance that this will probably result in some blisters, but I tell myself that I can take it.

Someone brings the Beast a stack of trays, but it isn't just a drop-off delivery. I could swear that the Beast has people practically bowing to him. I don't know how he does it, but somehow he seems to own this place. And while I am still at least a little petrified of this scary pirate, I can't help but be in awe of him too. I don't want to *be* him or anything, I can't even say for sure if I even like being around him, but I will admit that I think I'm safer with him than without him.

Deepvoice accepts the trays of food and carries them along. Our little entourage doesn't even stop to eat. We wait by the door until the buzzer opens it up.

Maybe it's the shower, or maybe it's just the break from cleaning dishes for the first time since I arrived, but I'm feeling the calmest I have ever been in here. I help Deepvoice unload as soon as we get back to the cellblocks. I even walk the Beast's dinner around to his cell. It's such a small thing, but somehow I feel like it means something to be allowed to help the almighty Beast. Tonight I'm the benevolent servant. I keep my head up, and try my best to let go of some of those chips on my shoulders – though I know it doesn't make up for my unnecessary surliness with Deepvoice earlier.

The Beast still mostly just grunts at me, but I've seen him do less, so I guess that's progress on both our parts. I set his tray down on a small metal table by his bed.

It's funny, we share the same bars, and yet that one silly little sheet-curtain does actually make it seem like we have a thick wall between us. I didn't even know that he had so much extra stuff in his cell. His bed is plush with bedding. He has several clothing items hanging around his bars. He's definitely been here long enough to make himself comfortable.

"Now what'ch'you after, boy?" he snarls. I guess he caught me looking. Even with one eye he still seems to see everything.

"Nothing," I say as reflex.

He snorts. He doesn't believe me.

"That's just your problem, boy. A man who ain't after nothing has nothing to live for."

"It's the Freakhouse," I say, "you can't get anything in here anyway."

"*Freakhouse*? I look like a *freak* to you, boy?"

I feel my throat dry up instantly.

"No, Sir. It's just… It's what we used to call it."

He's still glaring at me.

"The Institution. In my ward. We called each other Freaks."

"Green boys like you? And now you see where the real freakshow is, now, eh?"

"No, Sir – I mean, I don't think you're a Freak, Sir," I practically stutter.

"Your *'thinking'* hasn't done too well for you, now has it, boy?"

I bow my head. I can't save myself in front of him. It's better if I just shut up.

"Get on over to your side before you get locked out. I don't bunk with nobody. Especially not smartass green boys. Go on. Get!"

Well that's my benevolence all used up. I duck out and speed-walk around the row until I get to my side. It seems strange knowing that he's still just on the other side of that sheet. Really I haven't left him at all. At least not being able to see each other helps. I roll over on my bed. I still haven't replaced the sheet between me and Deepvoice. I wonder if he minds. Now there's a truly benevolent man. Makes me realize that I've pretty much been a total prick from day one. I hate that. If the guys from D46 saw who I was down here, they'd kick my ass.

But they did see it, didn't they? And the Skid. I lost it on all of them and Bear called me out on it.

I am ungrateful. I am selfish. The Beast knows it. Probably smelt it on me a mile away.

My tray is on the floor waiting for me. I pick at it more than I eat it.

I haven't really talked about my ward to anyone here. And with the way that time moves so slowly here, it feels like years since I've really talked to myself about it. I only seem to really remember the bad stuff. I only seem to remember my mistakes. It never really goes away.

I wake up to screaming. This one is even further away, but the jolt it sends through me as I think of Blue knocks me out of bed. I'm covered in tears and sweat. I hoist myself back up, grab the bunched sheet and stuff it over my ears. I want this to be done. I want it to stop.

I realize that I'm actually thankful for the shorter rest periods in my day. Being with myself in silence is unbearable. I would rather have the Beast belittle me with grunts and growls than have five minutes with my own broken self. At least when I'm busy some of the good memories creep in. All that the silence brings me is the stairwell. As much as I'm willing to let myself have it, seeing Blue mangled every time I close my eyes is not a torture I think I can live through.

"There's really no gettin' used to it," Deepvoice whispers to me. "Even the deepest sleeper among us can't ignore the *Taking*. Just try to think of somethin' good; it helps a little."

Something good. As if it were that easy.

"Anyone ever come back?" I ask.

"Mmhmm. It's been known to happen, and never for the better. Sometimes they's gone for weeks before anyone sees them again. Ain't nobody ever the same after. Don't know what's worse, the comin' back or the not."

"It happened to you?"

"No, sir. Lord only knows why. Ol' Joe ain't seen the white rooms neither. I guess we's too old for 'em to fuss about. But ol' Laz, they took him early on. No warnin', no 'xplainin', just gone in the night. Came back a good twenty days later, one leg on him. Few years gone by, they take him again. Carved him right up. Don't know what they took, but it came from the inside. Figure they got him harvesting."

"Harvesting?"

"A man's worth a whole lot if he's got the working parts. Figure that's what they keep us for. Just keeping the parts warm 'til they need 'em."

Somehow that seems rather fitting. I used to be afraid of what they might put in me, now they want me scared of what they might take away.

"I don't mean to scare you, boy," Deepvoice says sincerely.

"Don't worry," I tell him. "I already know what the White Coats are capable of. In my ward, they'd make us sick, just to see what would happen. I've seen kids swell up, shrink down, loose hair, grow hair, change colour; I've seen them breakdown, nearly kill themselves from the force of their own insides, from the pain they can't take anymore, from voices in their head that won't go away." I can still see Blue seizing in my bed. Marlene smashing her head into the floor.

I sit down just long enough to take a breath, and then I'm up on my feet again. If I sit, it *all* comes back. I've already let too much of it in. I haven't it in me to pace. I just cling onto the bars that separate us. Those bars are the safest thing to focus on.

"My… when they got their hands on him, he'd spell so bad, half the time I didn't think he'd ever recover… and then one day he didn't…"

"Ain't easy for nobody, I fear."

I can't talk anymore. I'm choking, even if it is silently. I don't want anyone to hear.

The screaming stopped a while back. There's nothing to stop anyone from hearing me. I pull the sheet over my head and rollover.

"Who was he?"

It's not Deepvoice. It's coming from behind me. The Beast was listening.

"The kid you saw die," he continues.

How can he ask me that?

"It doesn't matter," I spit out.

"Don't like names, do you, boy?"

"He was the only one who knew mine. I was the only one who knew his."

"And they killed the only person you ever trusted," the Beast guesses from behind the curtain.

"No… I did."

6

NAMES & NUMBERS

Dish duty has been quieter than usual, even though it wasn't the most conversationally fulfilling part of my day to begin with. I can never figure out what my cell neighbours are thinking. They haven't cut me out yet, but I have the feeling that they're second-guessing having included me in the first place. Even Deepvoice hasn't said a word to me since last night. Toothless is the quietest I've ever heard him; not a wheeze or a whistle.

If this is how it's going to be, I can brace myself for being cut loose. It's not like they owe me anything. To be honest, I'm surprised that they've kept me this long. I haven't exactly been the warm and friendly kind down here.

I won't dwell on the inevitable. I stay on task.

I'm getting much better at keeping up with the more seasoned guys beside me. I even manage to finish up my pile and do a basin dump before the buzzer sounds.

I meet up with my usual group, ready to pretend that nothing's changed. The Beast is handing out our lunch bags. I'm actually surprised to see that he's still made one for me.

"Thanks," I say briskly.

He glares at me. I don't know if I'm supposed to read this

one as worse than any other glare he's given me. I bow my head and just side inch my way closer to Deepvoice, ready to go on task.

"You're with me today, Kid," the Beast says, stunning me in place.

He takes a solid grip of his crutches and turns himself around. I look at Deepvoice. I don't know if I'm wanting his permission or his intervention. He gives me neither. The Beast is already making good speed. I have to catch-up, I have no idea where his actual task station is.

I jog up beside him. I want to ask him why I'm not going to the greenhouse, but I don't know if I'm going to like the answer. I'm kind of hoping that he'll just tell me if I need to know. I don't even know what his task is. I'm afraid to ask but I think it'll be worse not knowing. Either way I'm going to have to face it.

He's heading back towards the main building. We're far off from the pantry loading door, but I can still see it as we follow the walkway along the corner. There's a thick metal double door, the green paint mostly peeled away. I half expect this to be another storage room, but once inside it seems to be a transition room, only without the monitors. None of the doors have any sort of identifiers, and there's about five of them surrounding us.

"Where are we?" I can't help but ask.

The Beast doesn't stop. He goes right up to the door across from us, hooks his arm through his crutch so that he can reach the handle, and pulls it open.

No wonder he is always the one with the blankets; this is the fabric assembly room. Rows and rows of tables with old fashioned pedal sewing machines and even full size looms standing along the back walls.

"*This* is what you do every day?" I blurt out.

The Beast grunts. He heads down to an empty table and points to a stool for me to grab. There's already a stack of folded fabric waiting for him. I set the stool down beside him and wait for my orders.

"You know how to use this thing?" he asks me.

I have no idea which part of this whole mess he's asking me about so the safest and truest answer is just for me to shake my head.

He grunts and unfolds a portion of the fabric. He asks me to pass him a pair of very rustic looking scissors and then begins to cut away very selectively.

"What are we doing?" I ask, impatient for something to do aside from passing things based on varying tones of grunts.

"I make children's clothes. They go to the other wards," he says, almost proudly.

He has finished releasing his fabric and is now spreading it flat on the table carefully. It's like watching him kneed bread dough, only he's far gentler in smoothing this out.

"How did you get stuck with this job?" I immediately regret saying.

"I enjoy it well enough," he snarls. "I have two hands, may as well use them."

He's measuring now and making nicks with one edge of his scissors to mark his findings. He's so delicate, and it's so unlike anything I ever pictured him as that it takes everything I have to not laugh.

"You like sewing?" I ask.

"What can I say? I'm crafty." He still sounds pissed off, but he's also so focused. The dynamic of this bizarre scenario almost makes my brain hurt, and I guess it's made some part of it short-circuit because I can't believe that I'm still talking, and still smiling like an idiot.

"So what did you need me for?" I ask.

"Who said anything about *needing* you? Ain't anybody here *needs* you, kid. Never did."

"So why am I here?"

"That's exactly what I've been trying to figure out. Why are you here?"

"Because you told me to."

I think he just shot a dozen rounds into me from the harsh look he just gave me. I'm not smiling anymore.

"Start from the beginning," he orders.

I don't know how. I don't know where I begin.

"You're from the outside?" he asks, leading my own story on.

"Yes."

"Why'd they take you?"

"My mother died."

"And your father?"

"He was already in here."

"How old were you?"

"I was fifteen when they took me. Back in – "

"Fourteen," he answers before me.

How did he know that? I guess he could have done the math. I did tell Deepvoice about my Fresher year. It's only five years to calculate. He could have done that.

"It's on your wrist, boy," he says pointedly.

I look down. My barcode. 001014126. I see a fourteen, right in the middle.

"Ain't you ever noticed?" he asks me, finishing cutting out a small pair of pants. He pushes me back and slides himself into the pedal machine.

I stare at my code.

"I know my numbers," I say. "I guess I haven't really thought about what the rest of them mean."

"The rest of them?"

"Yeah. I like my twenty-six. It's my birthday."

"January," he says.

I look down at my wrist. Does it say that too? 1-26? Is that it? It can't be. Blue was 112. I know that. I remember that. He was a summer baby.

The Beast lays his wrist down across mine. I can see both of our codes now. 001094102.

"I'm a January, too," he says. "0-0-1. January 2nd. 0-2."

"And the middle? 0-1-4-1?" I ask, reciting my own code.

"Ignore most zeros. Everyone has them. Most people have that final one, too. 94; that's when they got me. 14; that's when they got you."

I slowly run my pinky finger over my number, revealing one number at a time. I've been staring at this number for the last five years. Blue had his since he was a baby. If he knew about it he certainly never told me. I'm trying to remember his now. I feel like if I can just put his numbers against mine, I'd know for sure. 007. I remember that. I remember the 7. 112. 7-12. July 12th. *Holy crap!* 007... I go through my numbers again. 001014126. 0070...

"You okay, there, boy?" the Beast asks me. I think he's genuinely concerned. "Didn't think you'd have an aneurism over it. It's just a label."

"How do you know that's what it is?"

He sort of grins. *Is that a laugh?* "Most folks will tell you the same. You just have to look. Different numbers, same pattern. Don't know why it is, just is. Makes it easy to tell us apart I suppose. Not unusual to have the same birthday as somebody else, or to be processed at the same time, but both is mighty rare."

I can't take my eyes off of my own wrist. I need to figure it out. I need to know the missing numbers. 0070...

"Arrival year?" I almost shout.

"What about it?"

Apparently my train of thought is hard to follow.

"That's the middle part?" I ask.

"It is for everyone I've met so far."

But... "What if you were born here?"

He gives me a look.

"What if you never arrived? What if you were born here?"

"I've never met anyone *born* on the inside. Is that even allowed? They breed you kids or something?"

I guess it never occurred to me that there weren't any women in this ward. I guess the thought of a co-ed arrangement might be hard to imagine. I guess making babies like Blue really couldn't happen down here.

"No," I say. Then I think about it. I think about Blue. I think about the library. I think about poor Marlene. It doesn't make me sad. It actually makes me laugh. If only I could have warned Marlene that I was never going to go all the way with her. "Some of us manage to, though."

This is a new look. It's not a scowl, but it might be irritated. I'm not sure if he wants to slap me. I watch his hands to see if they move. I might be safe.

"They don't separate us," I tell him. "We can't go into each other's rooms or anything, but anyone can find a way around that if they really want to."

I can't believe it. He actually does it. He actually laughs like a real normal person.

"And you let them take you out of there? You crazy, boy? I haven't even seen a woman since I got thrown in here. Whatever you did, you messed up bad, that's for sure."

You have no idea.

I trace over the numbers on my arm, replacing them with Blue's.

"The boy you lost?" he asks after finishing his third seam.

I cover my numbers and sit up straight.

"What is it that you need me do?" I ask, quickly changing the subject. "I should be doing something, right?"

"Need you to learn, boy."

I guess I should have been paying closer attention, like when he put my dinner in my cell.

"Sorry," I say.

"I'm not talking about this. I can't be bothered to teach you how to put two pieces together and I doubt you'd be any good at it. You've been in here for five years and somehow you've never learned how to survive. What're you going to do if I get *taken* in the night? Abe and Joe pass on in old age? You don't even know how to take care of yourself."

"I'm getting better."

"At what? Washing a few plates? Good on you, boy, but anyone here can do just as good if not better than you. You've got nothing worth having. No skills. No smarts. Hell, you ain't even got a name. How can anybody hope to trust you if you have no name? Can't tell someone that, what can you tell 'em? You'd be lost, boy, if it weren't for Abe and ol' Joe. You'd be lost if I didn't feed your sorry ass every day. You think you're in a bad place now? Remember that at any moment it can get a hell of a lot worse. They're always watchin', you know that, right? They see everything. You get useless, they put you to use. And you, boy, you've been useless since you dropped down into this place."

"Gee, thanks," I say stubbornly.

"I'm serious, boy. It's the hands or the mind. You make sure they know which one it is that you're keeping busy. You're new, they'll be watching you like a hawk. They don't care how sad you feel, how sore you are; they only see how much you're worth to them."

"I get it. Sit down, shut up, and keep working. Thanks."

"You make sure that's what they see. They believe what they see, boy, as most everybody does. They see you useless, they see you thinking, they see you're trouble."

"Okay, I get it," I say quickly.

"I don't think you do. You keep your hands busy, boy, but you keep that mind of yours turning too. It's the last thing they can take from you, boy, and believe me, they know how to take from a man." He swivels around so fast that it startles me. He takes both my wrists, holding them far too tightly, pressing his thumbs into my tendons. "What's your number boy?" he almost screams at me.

I don't know what the hell he's doing now. I'm practically shaking beneath him as he towers over me.

I recite dutifully, "0-0-1-0-1-4-1-2-6."

"And your name?"

I hesitate.

"Then you don't even know who you are," he says disappointedly. "And that boy who died, you know his name or his number?"

I know his name. I know his real name. I wish I could remember his number.

"You pouting because you lost him, or because you lost *you*?"

I don't know what to say. I don't know what it is that he

wants from me.

Apparently not much since the last thing he says to me is, "Get back to your garden."

I don't waste a single second. I bolt. It's not until I get outside that I let myself breathe.

I find Deepvoice in the corner, watering. I pretty much follow him around as I retell the whole weird exchange between the Beast and I. He doesn't react very much. I'm not even sure how much he's been listening to me.

"Well?" I ask.

"Well, what?"

"What do you think?"

"I think ol' Laz is tryin' to help you, boy."

That's not helpful.

"He's worried about you. We all are."

Still not helpful.

"You're young, boy. This place can take its toll on the best of us. And you're not ready to be down here with the likes of us. We a different breed down here."

"Yeah, I get that. You were transferred in."

"True, but we's also guilty. Not one of us didn't know what he was gettin' into. We didn't just drop down a hole and land here. We all knew it was coming. You, boy, you fell down one heck of a rabbit hole," he says, his belly laugh rolling out. "Bein' mournful and sorry for yourself don't help you climb back out – won't even get you back on your feet."

"I'm on my feet," I protest. "And I know my name. And I know B- "

Deepvoice stops and waits for me to finish. I can't do it.

"Why is *he* so obsessed with names?" I complain.

"Who?"

I know that he knows who I'm talking about, but he's watching me twitch trying to spit it out. I don't dare call him the Beast aloud, even if he isn't here to hear it.

"Laz," I finally say.

"Well now, that wasn't so hard, now was it?" Deepvoice says amusedly. "And he ain't obsessed. It's you, boy who's obsessed with not sayin' 'em. It's just plain unusual if you ask me, but to each his own. Things are sure goin' to get confusing around here when you ain't the baby in the cell no more. *'Which boy?' 'The nameless one.'*" He belly laughs again.

I don't join him.

"Sorry, boy. But we don't get many fun stories like that down here. Let an old man take what he can. In all seriousness, I wouldn't mind Laz too much. He's a bit rough around the edges, I'll be honest about that, and he's got good reason for it too, but he is right. You've got just the three of us on your team, boy. If you's stuck here, you's stuck with us, but we won't last forever."

"You mean I *am* stuck."

"You's as stuck as you make yourself, boy, that's all I'm sayin'."

The dishes pile up as usual, and I'm going full speed, muttering to myself, but thankfully if anyone can hear me, they don't seem to care. I'm breaking a strong sweat, trying not to think about the food I can smell. I just keep reciting numbers in my head. It was easy enough once I considered that Blue's entire birthdate would probably be used. He was two years older than me, the same as Jos, so I didn't even have to count to figure it out. 97. That's what I was missing. As I string together the numbers in my head, I can't believe that I didn't know it by heart before. 007097112. I've seen it so many times; I've heard it called out on the PA so many times. Over and over again I replay it in my head. It's almost musical. I know it's just a bunch of numbers, but I feel like I've accomplished something. 007097112. It flows nicer than my numbers. It fits. It's him. I can just picture him laughing at me for trying to hum out his barcode. He'd tell me that I was crazy and then tease me about it for weeks, but he'd be happy that I knew it. He'd want me to remember it.

I'm so focused that I don't even realize how long I've been working at the basins. The buzzer rings, that's what shakes me from my trance. Neither Deepvoice or Toothless are near me.

They might have gone to get their dinner sorted out. I hope that one of them has grabbed mine. I didn't even notice them wander off. Maybe they said something and I just didn't hear. Maybe they even tried to put something in front of me and I didn't even see it.

I drop what I'm doing and follow the herd out. I go straight to my cell and search every surface for where they might have put it.

I can't find it. Deepvoice isn't in his cell yet. Maybe they're still coming. I stand in the walkway, scanning faces as they pass by.

I spot Toothless. He's got a bowl full of scrambled eggs by the looks of it. He nods at me and then goes into his cell. I check Deepvoice's cell, even though there's hardly anywhere he could possibly hide himself within it, I just want to be sure that I haven't missed him.

No sign. I go around the back. Chances are that he's helping Laz with the carrying. Sure enough, even before I'm in front of the cell I can see bodies inside of it.

"Everything alright?" I try to say casually.

Laz keeps his eye on Deepvoice who does the same.

"That ol' alarm will be goin' off soon," Deepvoice says distractedly. "We should get movin'."

He picks up a larger plate. It's still steaming. I notice he's only picked up one. Laz is hunched over a bowl in his lap. I feel a lump in my throat. I follow Deepvoice out.

"What's going on?" I ask.

Deepvoice takes a moment. Hesitation. That's not a good sign. "Nothing for you to worry about. Ol' Laz just got himself worked up into one of his moods. I wouldn't mind him if I were you."

We get to his cell. He's being awfully quiet. I think I'm in trouble.

I let him go. I head towards my own cell.

"What in the world was I thinking?" Deepvoice suddenly exclaims as though he's had a life-changing epiphany, a very poorly acted life-changing epiphany. "Didn't even realize I was still carrying this. Sorry about that, boy." He's trying to smile as he scurries over to my door with his dinner.

It's sweet of him, but I know that one isn't mine. He's trying to give it to me, all of it. I can't take it. For as old as he is, for as hard as he's worked, for all that he's done for me, I can't steal his dinner too.

"We both know it's yours. You should eat.," I say.

"Oh I had my fill. Couldn't eat another bite if I wanted to."

Ol' Abe is a terrible liar; hard to believe that he could be a criminal – then again, this might be why he'd get caught.

I have no choice. I push him and his food out and shut my door. He looks more heartbroken about it than I am. It's better this way though. I take one of the sheets I've been using and take it over to our shared barred wall. He doesn't need to feel guilty about eating in front of me. It's not his fault. It's Laz who's trying to teach me a lesson. Let him. I'll figure it out.

I stand on the toilet bowl and start tying. It's harder doing the other side. I have to slide my foot up onto a horizontal bar in order to hoist myself up. I wobble a bit as I try to stretch out with the corner of the sheet, but I figure out how to do it with both hands if I wrap my arm around a bar and hold it snug in the crook of my elbow. I get it up, but from here I can still see into Deepvoice's cell. He's just watching me, looking sad. I let go, jump down, and try not to think about it.

I fill my drinking cup with water and set it next to my bed. I don't even lie down, I just sit, hunched over, staring at nothing at all. I see the twin markings on my wrists. I recite Blue's numbers in my head again. 007097112. I feel my feet tapping with the rhythm I created. 007097112. I'm tracing it out on my wrist, just below my own. 007097112. Over and over again. 007097112. 007097112. 007097112.

I don't notice the sting until the blood begins to pool. It fills up the 9 until it is indistinguishable, then it pours over the others. I don't have anything to wrap it in, nothing that I'd want to use anyways, so I run it under the tap for about a minute. I feel the sting now.

When I bring my hand away, I can see the new markings.

The numbers aren't straight, but they're there. It starts to pool again, but at least more slowly this time. I read it over. I can hear Blue's voice. *Don't leave me.*

I lay down, keeping my bleeding hand above my head just to stop the temptation I have to start rubbing it. I close my eyes. I can almost smell him. I can almost feel that fluff of hair of his. I put my own arm across my waist. It doesn't feel the same, but it's something. If he were here, he'd be this close to me. I'd keep him this close to me. I'd never let him go.

7

DOWN & UP

I don't remember falling asleep, but I hear the buzzer and know that I'm awake. My door is now unlocked and open. I'm slow to get up. Before I'm even in a sitting position, I notice that Deepvoice is standing at my door, a piece of oatcake in his hand.

"Good morning," I say groggily.

"Thought you could use this," he says, inching his way closer to me.

I know that he won't stop until he sees me eat something. I feel less guilty about this because I know that he'll be well taken care of for breakfast.

I thank him and reach for it. His whole body freezes for an instant, it's unreal, like someone just pressed a pause button. Then I realize what he's staring at. My bloody wrist probably suggests a far worse story than what actually belongs to it.

"Don't worry about it," I say and switch hands.

He drops the oatcake into my right hand. I let him see me take a bite. The relief washes over his face like I would never have thought possible.

"You going to tell me what happened to that there arm of yours?" he asks me cautiously.

I don't know if I should cover it up or just let him see it.

"Just remembering," is all I say.

"I ain't never seen no folks remember quite like that. You thinkin' on sad things?"

I nod slowly, and take another bite. "Some good things too," I add after I've swallowed.

I decide to show him. Some of the blood has crusted overtop of the numbers so you can't read them, especially the nine in the middle, but it seems like Deepvoice understands enough of it.

"That boy of yours?" This is the second time someone's brought it up. I know I'm the one who first mentioned it, but it still seems weird to have someone else talk about it – about him.

"I figured out the numbers. I remembered them. Didn't want to forget again," I say, trying to sound more cool about it than mournful, as Laz accused me of.

Deepvoice doesn't ask me anymore about it. He lets me get ready on my own and I walk to the kitchen hall by myself. I could have gone straight to the basin, but I had to set something straight first. I go right up to Laz's counter and set myself directly beside him.

"What do you want from me?" I ask him immediately. "I was asked to contribute, and from day one I've done that. You told me to do dishes; I've been doing dishes; I've been doing dishes every goddamn day!"

He doesn't say anything. He's hardly even looking at me.

"You're more than your job, boy. You're too young and too inexperienced on the outside to know that yet. You'll figure it out."

"This is still about my name, isn't it?" I say accusingly. "Call me whatever the hell you want, I don't care. A name's no more a part of me than the shirt on my back. You gave me this one, why not a name too?"

"You think too much, boy, but not on the important

things. It's going to get you in trouble one day."

I exhale loudly.

"Am I getting my own food today? That's all I want to know," I finally say.

He's still not looking at me.

"If you can get it, by all means, get it."

I trudge off, irritated as hell. I guess it's out of habit, but I walk back to my dishes. I know I can't go till the buzzer if I want to gather enough for breakfast and lunch. I don't even have a bundle since I never got mine back yesterday. I hope that there's something I can use in the pantry or something I can borrow from someone else. I glance around me every few minutes just to see if there's anyone I feel like I could approach.

I hate to admit it, but something about what Laz has said to me is starting to make sense. Aside from that small group, I have nothing to do with anyone else in this prison. I may have only been close to a few people in my old ward, but I knew lots of people, I knew their names, their personalities, I knew who I'd rather be working beside while on task, who I could trust to help me with something… Even worse, I don't even want to have that here. I don't want to get comfortable. I don't want to be close. He was right – I'm not going to last long in here.

I gauge my time as best as I can. I still have plenty of dishes piled up at my basin, and I want to get them done, if nothing else, just for that small feeling of accomplishment even though I know perfectly well that my job is never-ending and, really, in the grand scheme of things, I've accomplished nothing. I tell myself that I can get through just a few more. Just a few more. This one last one.

Crap! Buzzer!

I throw down the bowl in my hand and practically jump over my station to get to that pantry. People are moving in and out, trying to put leftovers away or cart out the few things that they need. I try to quickly scan for something I can take, but it's hard to tell what's what. Most things are placed inside boxes or cloth bags. There are no labels. I guess if you were used to where everything went, you wouldn't need to read a label. I have no choice but to do some rummaging.

I'm trying to be careful – I don't actually want someone to think that I'm stuffing my face this whole time. I just need a few pieces to get me through: bread, cheese, an apple or two. I don't even care if I find any of the dry meat; I need sustenance, not luxury.

The bread is easy enough to find. It's laid sparingly spread out with small cloths loosely draped over top. All bread is made as small rolls so I don't feel too selfish grabbing one.

"What'ch'ya doin', Kid?" someone asks me.

A group of four are bringing in a full roast pig. It's tempting, but I wouldn't even have time to carve into it, let alone survive the attempt with these guys standing over me. This must be the last to come in. I don't have much time.

"I missed my pack lunch," I tell them – it's mostly an honest answer.

"Hurry it up. Grab an apple and go."

What a godsend! The guy points to a covered stack.

I rush over, and sure enough, under the sheet are barrels of apples. I know I don't have time to continue the hunt, so I grab three of them. I do feel a bit guilty – apple season won't be prime until the fall and our greenhouse stock is precious until then, but it's that or starve – or be locked –

Crap! Buzzer!

The four guys are nowhere in sight. I try to bolt for the door but somehow I trip. My foot's caught a loop of the apple tarp. Not only have I tumbled, but at least two barrels have come down with me. They don't land on me or anything, but that crashing sound makes me shudder. I do not want to be the one responsible for two barrels worth of bruised apples. I scramble to my feet and quickly try to at least put the barrels upright again. I know I don't have time to chase rolling fruit, so I accept that failure and just focus on getting out of the pantry – out of the kitchen is more like it.

Then I hear it, the final click. I'm surprised that the pantry door hasn't slammed shut in front of me, but I'm not exactly disappointed about that. There's no point in me running out to the doors at the far end. I know they're locked and I'd rather not draw attention to myself as being a stowaway. Even if all of the prisoners are gone, there's still those cameras that I don't need to see me singled out. I do have another shot though. The connecting door between the pantry and the loading dock. They'll be opening that back door soon enough, maybe not right away, but soon, if I wait in there I should be able to get back out into the yard. I can't be the first guy to have not made it out in time. I'm just thankful that I didn't end up shut in the showers.

It's a clear path to the door. I pretty much throw myself against it as I grab the handle. It won't move. This is so stupid! I get that it needs to be locked to prevent food lines during the day, but damn it, why not make it a one-way lock!

I'm so screwed. My only salvation is that I'm trapped with food. I plop on the floor and take up one of the apples from the ground. I dropped my savings rushing to the locked door, not that it matters now. There's no use in panicking. I just eat. If I'm going to be in here a while, I might as well get familiar with the place. I stay seated but I take my time eying the different shelves and what's standing in front of them. It's become much easier to assess what might be lurking behind wrappings now that I don't have a ticking clock in the back of my brain. Based on where the pig was placed, I take a pretty decent guess at where the other meat is. Beside that I'm pretty sure is the cheese. I wonder how long all of this will last. It's cool in here, that's for sure, but it certainly isn't a fridge of any sort. I suppose with all of these mouths, it must get rotated frequently enough.

I look to see if there's any controlling the temperature in the room – not that I want to mess with it, I'm just curious if anyone has a say in it at all.

It doesn't look promising. I don't see any switches, only the pull cord for the lights. Above me there's only one vent. It must be linked to air conditioning of some sort, though it isn't blowing down very hard.

A smirk comes across my face as I think about it. If Blue were here he would be up in that vent in ten seconds flat. There wasn't anywhere he hadn't explored in our old ward; if he were here, exploring would be the first "to-do" on his list. A vent like that probably wouldn't lead to anywhere very interesting. It probably connects to the main cellblock, the kitchen, and maybe a few side rooms –

Side rooms? Staff rooms? Labs? Control centre?

All I can see now is that faithful mischievous smirk on Blue's face, his eyes all lit up in bright blue, his greyish eyebrows perked up. *"Come on!"*

When could I ever resist that devilish grin?

I examine the vent door as best as I can from down here. It just looks like it's held together by basic screws. I just need something thin enough to fit. I'm surrounded by food; not helpful. I know that just beyond that open door is a whole kitchen full of utensils. Something out there has to fit. I don't know if I want to risk it though. If someone notices that I'm in here, even if I do get that vent open, I'm sure there are only so many places I could possibly be. Unless this thing magically transports me to the outside, outside of the entire county, I'll be picked up in no time.

"Come on. Trust me."

I might as well see if it's even worth it.

I check how sturdy the shelving unit is. It's free-standing, but hopefully if it's this loaded up, I can still get up there.

I psych myself out the first few times, barely even lifting both feet off of the ground. The shelving doesn't wobble or anything, so really I shouldn't be so chicken about it. I wish that I could just walk out into that kitchen hall. I could get a knife, a stool, and hell, maybe no one would even notice. Maybe this prison block runs itself so well that no one checks up on it so long as the stock is handed over every day.

I still don't know if I want to risk it.

What's the worst that could happen? I'm already at Ground Zero – they literally have nowhere else to put me. I mean, they could always leave me in a lab with Parish where he could give me some sort of incurable form of malaria or just saw off my legs like they did with Laz. I know that I can't pull off many more escape attempts if I have no legs.

What was it that Laz said? *"If you got hands, use 'em?"* Something like that anyways.

I look down at my wrist. Blue's numbers practically glow off of my arm. Soaking in dishwater removed most of the crusted blood. Even the 9 is clear, red, but clear. He'd do it. Blue would risk it for an adventure.

"You better be with me on this," I say to him.

I jump onto the first shelf.

It's holding so far. I go real slow in climbing up to the next one.

Not even a wobble. One more.

I don't look down. I feel like I can almost reach it. One more.

It's an awkward angle but I could in theory get to two of the screws, maybe three if I really pushed myself, and four if I had a bungee cord as a precaution. I feel the closest screw with my thumb nail. It's tight. That screw probably hasn't been moved in years. I wouldn't be surprised if it was rusted into place. I definitely need a tool of some sort.

I descend and consider my options one more time.

I get low on the floor and peek my head out of the doorway. I don't see a camera, and I can't imagine that the Institution would bother with super-secret hidden ones. My old ward was rolling in the expensive equipment compared to this place, and even us inmates knew where all of the cameras were. I crawl a little more forward, just so that I can get beyond the open door.

I see it. I'm surprised. *Just one?* They really don't care what goes on down here, do they? I guess one is all you need if a huge brawl breaks out or someone dies… or someone gets left behind. It doesn't look like it moves at all. It's stuck in the corner with a decent eagle-eye view of the massive hall. With all of the tables, stands and islands, it's hard to tell if I'll be covered at all. The biggest issue is the initial open space in front of me.

I look down at my wrist one more time. "If this goes sideways I'm blaming you," I tell him.

I've made up my mind. Quick, low, small. I just need to get over to one of the basins. That's not too far away, and when I get there I'll be covered pretty well. I scrunch myself up, resting on my ankles. I take a deep breath and pounce. I'm on my hands, still scrunched up, running my little feet like they are on fire. I launch myself beneath the nearest basin stand.

I realize that I probably didn't pull this off nearly as smoothly as I had originally pictured it in my mind, but I made it this far, that's all that really matters.

I crawl down the length of the basins. Nearer the end are the piles of to-be-washed dishes. Grabbing from there is probably safer than reaching up for something that might not even be in that basin. I could go all down the line and not find what I'm looking for. At least down on the floor I can see what's in this pile. I carefully pick through and find a knife. I slip it out and scurry back. I have to talk myself into crossing that big open space again, but I tell myself that when you consider the open door, it actually isn't all that far of a distance.

As prepared as I can be, I scrunch up and scurry back. I don't launch myself to the ground until I know I'm well inside the pantry. I don't want to risk being caught out just because my feet stick out somewhere for too long.

No alarms have been sounded so I take that as a good sign. I'm starting to like this, never needing to scan myself in. No remembering alarm cues, no blaring warnings or fake salutations. I guess there are some perks to being down here.

I stand up, check over my chosen instrument, glad not to have broken it already, and start my climb again. This is far more awkward, having to not only wield something while hanging on for dear life, but to actually wield it in a coordinated enough fashion so that it's actually useful.

It seems to be taking forever just to make the screw move

even a tiny bit, but once I manage to get one good full turn, it comes out like nothing at all. The second one is just as stubborn, but I'm more confident that I can make the damn thing move now and it seems to go faster. With the two screws gone, the vent cover droops down. I pull at it to see if I really need to get those other two screws out. The moment I tug it down, one at the far end pops right off, broken in half. *That was easy.* I need to get just a little bit higher if I'm going to pull myself into the vent.

I grab onto the rim as best as I can as I try to bring one foot up to a higher shelf. I already feel like I'm being pulled in too many directions, and if I bring up my other foot, I'm sure I'm going to topple over. If I'm going to do it, I just need to launch myself – I seem to be doing that a lot on this mission I made for myself.

I count to three aloud and then push off, leaping towards the opening, trying to ram my elbows securely inside so that I can wriggle up. I barely fit and have to tuck my shoulders through one at a time – and endure much scrapping of the skin even through my shirt – but once my upper half is in, I can propel myself well enough to crawl up.

Once I make it all the way in I realize that I hadn't really considered how I was going to get back down again. Trying to swing for the shelving again seems like a longshot in multiple ways. I guess this is just more motivation to push forward.

If there's one good thing about cheap homemade clothing, it's the lack of buttons and zippers. Nothing catches, nothing clangs, I just wriggle right down. I pass a few openings, all of which are within the cell block. I have no desire to go crashing down over a locked cell. It's not even as though I could drop inside of a cell, they have high barred tops, I guess for this very reason. If I thought that I could have climbed my cell wall to get to a vent system, I would have done it on the first day, as I'm sure hundreds of other prisoners would have thought too. At least in the pantry you aren't staring up at the ceiling everyday seeing temptation calling you.

This might be a fool's errand. There might not be any

openings once I get across the cell block. I don't know how many more I'm going to come across before I reach the end of the block. I know the place is huge, but I've never actually seen the walls on both ends. I have no idea how many rows I'd need to pass over. But I've got nothing else to do, so I keep going.

The view changes. I get to an opening and it doesn't look like the cell block at all. It's a stairwell. I have no idea where I am or if I'll have to face being scanned in this part of the Institution. I know that the stairwell Blue and I hung-out in would let us go up and down for who knows how many floors, the only thing stopping us were the monitors and the potential for traffic. I think about taking my chances, but the vent has a few options for going upwards. I might as well see what's up before I hit the stairs.

Up is much harder. I put cramps in my feet trying to hold myself in place as I squirm along, pulling myself up by the sheer strength of my fingers. Not fun, but at least there's no impending-doom slice-and-dice fan beneath me like the movies always put in, so that takes some of the pressure off.

I couldn't be more relieved to get onto a flat landing. I wriggle along, trying to navigate away from the staircase so that I can actually see what's on this floor. It should be the main floor, which will be interesting because the first thing you see when you walk into the building are the elevators. I don't even remember seeing side offices when I first arrived – then again, I wasn't exactly taking careful notes while being dragged through.

I certainly didn't expect to find *that*. Beneath me seems to be a plastic jungle gym. I don't hear anyone, and I don't see anyone – not that I have much of a range from this tiny box I'm in. I push down on the vent cover. There's no way that I can unscrew it from the outside, and as much as I might like to, kicking it down is probably not the smartest option, if any of what I'm doing could possibly be listed in the "smart" category.

I feel for the tip of one of the screws and see if I can move it from here. It's tight, or maybe my hand is sweaty, but once I position it between my knuckles instead of my fingertips, I get it to move. This is actually much easier to do while lying over top of the cover than what I had to do climbing up the stupid food shelf, dangling like a monkey.

I get the screws free and gently twist the cover so that I can bring it up here with me. I peek down.

It's a playroom. There are three of these jungle gym setups, scattered toys and pretend house tri-folds. I look for a camera, but I don't see one. I guess with kids this little, they need more hands-on supervision than the nanny-cam type they give us.

I turn myself around and let myself down. This is a very strategically placed jungle gym. I can easily climb back up into my new secret passageway from here. I stay low, just in case, and scan the area. There's only one door, and by the look of it, it's operated by a card scan. On one hand that's good for me because I don't run the risk of having one of my barcodes read. On the other hand, I have no way out of this room unless someone comes in. I don't really want someone to come in – that would be bad.

There's nothing I can do in here so I pull myself back up. I leave the cover off. If these kids are that small, they won't reach it, and I doubt any of them would really care. I doubt I would have as a kid.

I keep crawling along. I stop at every potential opening just to see what's there. It's all the kids' ward, the one Blue would have grown up in.

I crawl over what look like classrooms – at least from what I remember kindergarten classrooms to look like – and see that lessons are being taught. Kids are singing songs, being read to, or working somewhat quietly. I guess it all depends on their age. That was one similarity, most of the kids seem to be grouped fairly close in age, at least there didn't seem to be a noticeable age gap from my not-so-brief lingerings.

I pass over a baby nursery that I heard long before I ever reached it, and for these last few openings it's been a massive group bedroom. Rows of bunk-beds, just like my old ward, only there are dozens in this room. I find myself so absorbed in watching this new world beneath me that I don't feel like I am passing through a living world that could actually see me. That is until I see another set of eyes staring back at me.

She screams. I want to too, but I do everything I can to try to get her to calm down. A little girl had been lying peacefully on her top bunk until I strolled over scaring her half to death. She stops screaming as she enters a coughing fit.

"Are you okay?" I ask her.

I can't tell if she's hyperventilating or choking. I don't hear anyone else, and I imagine that if someone else were in the room, they would have said something at the first sign of screaming. I just react. I kick the vent cover off and plop down beside her. She's making wheezing sounds.

"It's okay, just put your head back a little," I tell her. "Try to breathe slowly through your nose."

I breathe with her until she stops panicking.

"Better?" I ask.

She nods.

"I'm sorry, I didn't mean to scare you."

She's still drawing long slow breaths.

"Why are you in my ceiling?" she asks.

Her face is becoming less red. She's much calmer.

I could try to explain myself to an eight year old, but I don't even know how I'd put it into words to an adult. The engraved numbers on my left arm inspire me. What would Blue tell her?

"I'm exploring."

She looks at me skeptically. "In the ceiling?"

"Have you ever been up there?" I ask her, letting myself be playful about it.

She shakes her head.

"Shouldn't someplace you've never been be explored?"

"I guess."

"So I'm exploring."

"I don't think you're allowed to do that," she says.

I can tell that she's going to grow-up to be one of those book-smart tattletale girls one day. I hope she's not too set on the tattling yet.

"Maybe *you* aren't," I try to say teasingly.

It's been so long since I've been around a little kid, I don't know how well I'm doing. For all I know I'm coming off as one of those creepy guys who hangs around school yards in windowless vans. I guess dropping out of the ceiling into a little girl's room isn't much better.

"Why aren't you with the others?" I continue. "Are you allowed to be here by yourself?"

She nods.

"I'm sick," she says. "I don't have to go."

"You're sick? How did that happen?"

She shrugs her shoulders.

They shouldn't be altering kids this young. I see that she only has one brand, her left wrist. They'll take care of her, at least I hope that they would. She's still technically eligible to be fostered out; she's the type of inmate that they'll actually let the public and business partners see. No one can resist a happy healthy child when it comes to sponsorship.

I pick up the vent cover. I've put a lot of dust in her bed. Definitely not good for a kid who's already sick. I tuck the metal frame back up into the opening.

"Are you going to explore again?" she asks me.

She's adorable, but I have to remind myself that she could tell on me at any moment.

"You don't want me kicking around here if you're sick. You were probably trying to sleep, weren't you?"

She shakes her head. "I'm tired of sleeping."

Ha. I know what that's like.

"It's all I'm allowed to do," she adds. "It's so boring. And no one even talks to me because they think that they'll get sick too."

"How long have you been sick?" I ask.

She shrugs. "Too long."

Good answer.

"What's your name?" she asks me.

How often have I been faced with this question? But she's a sick little girl. I hardly even need to think about it. I tell her.

"Blanky."

She giggles a little, and then coughs a lot. She recovers.

"That's a funny name."

I shrug modestly. "What can I say, I'm a funny guy."

She tries not to giggle. I know I shouldn't be trying to make her laugh, but I need her not to be scared of me.

"Is that really your real name?"

She's a tricky one.

"Of course it is. Why wouldn't it be?"

"Because it's not a real name!"

I pretend to be offended. "Is too!"

She giggles.

"Alright smartypants, what's *your* name?"

She pulls the blanket she's sitting on up to her chin. "Beth."

"*Bath*? What? Is that like short for Bathtub? And you say that I don't have a real name. That's just weird."

She's all giggles now, even as she's getting a little mad. "No! BETH!"

"I heard you. I got it," I say. "Just Bath, no tub."

"No! BETH! BEH-TH!"

"Bath-tub."

"No!" She plops over.

Even I'm laughing too much now. But she starts coughing again and I know I have to stop. Her face is going red, and you can hear how clogged up her chest must be if she's coughing that deeply. I try to hush her and rub her back a little. She spits up into her hand. I wish I had something to give her, but she's already pulling a tissue out of her pocket. She cleans herself up a bit and then rubs her chest where it must hurt.

"I'm sorry," I say. "I should go."

"I'm okay," she says.

"And you'll be even better if I don't get you riled up." I take her pillow and shake it out over the side of the bed, then I hand it to her and roughly try to push away the clumps of dust on her bed sheets. "There you go," I say, "a bit better, eh?"

She looks so sad now.

"I don't want to sleep!"

"You don't have to sleep, you just gotta take it easy. A bit hard to do with funny guys like me dropping out of your ceiling, huh?"

She pouts and shakes her head.

"I won't laugh," she promises.

"That'll be hard to do around me, Bathtub; I even look funny."

She smiles but keeps her lips clamped tight, trying to prove that she can do it. Got to admire her spunk at such a young age.

"When do the others come back?" I say, willing to compromise a bit.

"Not until after lessons. But Miss Aidle brings me lunch so that I don't have to go to the lunch room."

"When's that?"

She turns to the monitor at the foot of her bed, similar to the ones we had in our ward, and turns it on. It's the first time I've seen a clock since I went to the prison. It's only 8:30am. Beth tells me that lunch always comes at noon. I've got a couple hours.

"She ever check up on you before then?" I ask her.

She shakes her head.

"Don't worry," she says, "I won't let them find you."

That catches me off-guard. She's a smart kid – well, unless you factor in that I'm technically a jail-break criminal. I mean, I know that I'm okay, but this little girl is awfully trusting.

I'm hesitant, but she's looking up at me with these huge baby blue eyes – I can't say no.

I guess she figured out that I was caving because she lit right up and practically bounced right down her side ladder.

"Where're you going?" I ask.

"Come here!"

I have no choice. I hop down. She's skipping over to an activity centre. It's an area outlined by large rugs, surrounded by tables, stacked drawers, bean bag cushions, shelves of books and toys, everything a kid could possibly need. How was she *so* bored?

She sits at one of the tables and tells me to join her. She hands me a stack of paper. At least this doesn't involve dolls. She's amazingly focused as she picks through the colours she wants out of old tin cans. I can see as she begins to draw that she takes her art very seriously. Me, not so much. I take the tin of crayons and have a go at my typical colouring template: red house on a green hill with a blue sky. I haven't played with colours in years. I feel a little bit like an idiot to tell the truth, but I also feel remarkably free. How in the hell did I get myself into a situation in which I can just sit and colour with an eight year old?

We sit there for hours just colouring. She tells me stories about the other kids, and I make terrible jokes. It's great. Though nothing quite beats having access to a bathroom that actually carries toilet paper. I am tempted to take a roll out of one of the stalls and carry it back with me – just to keep in my cell for my morning and evening use. But, of course, all it would take is for someone to notice my little luxury and I'm sure that I'd have plenty of explaining to do.

When I return from the bathroom, she shows me the last picture she was working on. She's drawn a man in a cape flying like Superman.

"Hey, that's pretty good," I tell her.

"It's you," she says. "But without *this*." She takes hold of my wrist. I don't know if she means my barcode, or my mutilation. I'm sure either is fair game. "I hate them," she says suddenly very serious. "Will they give me another one? I heard that they do. I've seen grown-ups with them, like you. Do they hurt?"

"You have one," I remind her, holding her hand, "you tell me."

"I don't remember. I was too little."

I kneel down to her. "You've been here a long time, huh?"

She nods, keeping her eyes down as if she's ashamed of it.

"It's okay. Me too."

She looks up. She's almost crying. I can see that she's trying not to.

I touch her face, pull her dark blonde hair behind her ears. "You've got nothing to be scared of."

I don't even feel like I'm lying. I wouldn't have said it if I thought she'd be taken down to Ground Zero, but she'll get a good ten years out of my ward with nothing to worry about.

She starts coughing.

I rub her back until she recovers.

"What's this one?" she asks, careful not to touch the redness on my wrist.

I don't even know how to begin to explain this one. I breathe out slowly, trying to put some words together in my head.

"It belongs to a friend of mine. I didn't want to forget him. Pretty silly, huh?"

She examines it. "Does it hurt?"

"Not as much as you might think." I don't want to tell her that I'm going through a bit of a sadistic phase and actually feel better knowing that it's there, etched into me, that it's worth whatever pain it has caused me.

She drops my arm and runs away.

Great! Now I've freaked her out!

Just as quickly, she comes back to me, takes up my hand again, and begins to write with the pen she retrieved. Just below Blue's number, I see that she's written out another one. 005009122.

"Now you won't forget me either," she says.

I take the pen from her and write awkwardly with my left hand on my right wrist. Just beneath my barcode, I scrawl "Bathtub" and show her.

"Definitely not forgetting this," I say.

She smiles but is trying to make an angry face at the same time.

At 11:30am I tell Beth that I have to go. She pouts, but it's clear she knows that I can't be here when her lunch is delivered. I climb back on her bed and pull myself into the vent.

"Will you come back?" she asks, staying as close to my feet as she can.

I pull my legs up and turn myself around. Popping my head down, I say, "No promises. I don't know if I'll get another chance. But, if I can, I definitely will."

She smiles. I guess that's good enough for her. "When?" she asks so full of hope.

"I don't know," I reply honestly. I think about how much longer I have to wait before anyone else in the prison will be let back in. I've got hours still to kill. "I'll be around, though, don't worry."

"You won't forget?"

I show her my wrist as a reminder to her.

"Good," she says.

8

BLANKET

It's a ridiculously long time before the buzzer sounds. I have been curled up on the pantry floor, wrapped in the apple tarp, waiting. Luckily there was enough time to put the barrels back in order so all I had to do when I woke up from my nap was toss the sheet back over it. Now that I hear the doors unlocking, I allow myself to stroll out into the kitchen. Better to be found out there than in here.

I have hardly eaten anything all day, just those few pieces I gathered for myself earlier. A small roll and a few apples definitely didn't fill me up any, but I can't handle just taking more food like this. Everyone else worked their asses off today. I may have had a small adventure of my own, but aside from major discomfort, a few scrapes, and being scared out of my mind that I was going to die, get caught, or get stuck and then subsequently die very slowly, my troubles were pretty minimal. Besides, I made a new friend today.

For the first time in a long time, I actually felt a little more like my old self while in the children's ward – a little more like Blanky. I haven't been him since I lost Blue. I suppose that's why I've been feeling so empty. I didn't just lose my best friend, but I lost the best part of me, too – the part that cared

83

about anything or anyone. I don't know what that's left me, but it hasn't been good. It hasn't been good for anyone.

I should have had a better first meeting with Luke, the new Skid roommate who came in just a few days before I got myself thrown down here. I must have traumatised that poor kid. It wasn't at all how I wanted it to go down. It wasn't what the kid deserved. At least he's in better hands now. Froggy and Bear, my friends, my Freak brothers, they'll take good care of him.

I try to picture what D46 might be like now, now that I'm gone too. They'd have a new roommate. Another Skid, probably a kid from below. From what I saw crawling around, there's no shortage of kids in the Freakhouse.

Funny that I'd think of it as that again. *Freakhouse*. Even funnier is that that's somehow comforting to me. I keep thinking about it as I prepare my basin. I have to change the water out. I'm already at it as people start strolling in.

I stay dead silent and work almost robotically. I try to maintain a steadily rapid pace even with keeping my left hand out of the water as much as I can manage. It's inevitable that the pen marks will fade away sooner or later, and "Bathtub" is easy enough for me to write out again, if I ever get near another pen, but numbers are trickier. I try not to stare at my own wrist while on task. I know that I'm tempted to, but I have a whole night to get through still, and probably a very hungry one too.

"You here, boy!" Deepvoice cries out. He pats my shoulder. "Ain't nobody seen you. Thought you got yourself snatched-up. Where've you been?"

"Keeping busy," I say quietly.

"I've been askin' all around. Ain't nobody knew where you'd gone. I thought you'd be with Laz when you ain't shown up to the greenhouse. Just to be curious, I took myself on a bit of a stroll, and he ain't seen you neither. Checked with ol' Joe, too. You do look worn, boy. Where'd you go?"

I don't want to lie to him, but I also don't want the whole world to know. I'm practically shoulder to shoulder with others along the dish line, and I don't want anyone to think that I've been sneaking around or trying to dodge out.

"I'll tell you a story later," I say, a little smirk on my face so he knows not to worry.

I can see his eyebrow rise up. He's ready to be let in on the joke, but it's obvious that he's just glad that I'm alright.

I power through my dishes. The pile I'm making in the rinse-water tub beside me is almost ready to topple back into mine. I walk briskly to dump out my water – running with a full tub of water just makes a ridiculous mess. When I come back to the station I see another row back-logged. I'm feeling good, and I'm liking this fast pace I'm moving at, so I jump over.

"Want an extra hand?" I ask, but I've already plunged in.

The puffy-faced guy manning the basin stares skeptically at me for a few seconds, makes a sound that reminds me of a dog sneezing, and then backs off a little to make room for me. I have my own rag so the work goes by quick, at least for me. I can see that his fat, possibly swollen, fingers don't give him much dexterity. Trying to get between a stubborn piece, like a fork, must be hell for him. I take it upon myself to dig for the cutlery and let him handle the big pieces. I don't know if he noticed or not, but it did bring him up to speed better.

We don't get through it all by the time the buzzer sounds. I didn't really expect to. I had only been there a few minutes anyways. I quickly filter through to find any other pieces waiting beneath the murky water and dig them out. I offer to dump his basin. He gives me that same skeptical look, but then put his hands up as a "be my guest" sort of gesture.

I drop the empty basin back on its stand, toss his cloth in it, and then throw mine into my own station. There is still a sizable swarm piling out of the hall, so I slip in with them and pool out into the cell block.

I see right away that Deepvoice is waiting at my cell door. He's got a bundle wrapped around his arm and a bowl in his hand. I'm already sighing and shaking my head before he can even see me.

"I'm not taking your food," I tell him as I walk directly past him.

He follows me sternly and puts both items on my bed.

"I ain't givin' you my food, boy."

It's my turn to look skeptical.

"You missed every meal today. How've you been gettin' on?"

He unwraps the bundle. It's extra full, I'm guessing because he's put my breakfast in there too.

"Wasn't sure if I earned my handouts today," I confess. "Took a couple of apples. It's got me through the day."

"Apples and oatcake ain't enough to live on, boy."

I agree and then ask him where his dinner is, just to be safe. He lifts up the partitioning sheet and points out the unmistakable plate of beans, potatoes and thin ham slices.

"Fair enough," I say after receiving my proof.

I go after the hot food first. I know I won't eat the bundle all tonight, but it'll be good to have some extra on hand.

Deepvoice watches as I shovel in my first bite with my fingers. "Now, are you goin' to –"

He's going to ask me about my adventure, he's stopped because I have a new visitor. I wouldn't have noticed if he hadn't have paused so unexpectedly.

It's the puffy-faced man from the kitchen. I don't know how he found my cell – maybe he just followed me. Nevertheless, he's standing at my door, his own dinner plate in hand.

Once he's been acknowledged, he lets himself in. Doesn't say a word. He walks right up to me, almost toe to toe as I'm sitting on my bed, frozen in place.

He turns his plate down and flips one of his ham slices into my bowl. Still not a word.

"Thanks," I say, "but – "

He raises his hand. He's taking command.

"You work, you get paid," he says sternly. "Reuben doesn't make debts, and he doesn't collect them."

I don't know what to say. I was about to say "thank you"

again, but he twitched his face just as I opened my mouth like he knew it was coming and was telling me to shut-up.

"I'll be sure to remember that... Reuben?" I didn't mean for it to sound like a question, but I wasn't sure what he'd let me say so I spoke slowly waiting for another face twitch.

"Your name, boy?"

I could have hit my head against the wall. *Why is it always this question?* I looked over at Deepvoice who was already shaking his head as if he could already hear my side of the conversation taking place; maybe he was also imagining how a big guy like Reuben would pummel a tiny guy like me into the ground in much the same way that the Beast kneads his bread.

I don't feel like fighting or arguing. Besides, I told Beth I'd find a way to see her again and I can't do that if I'm dead, or a vegetable.

I sigh – finally defeated.

"Dotan, but most people call me Blanky."

The look on Deepvoice's face is priceless. I think *he's* the one at risk of being in a state of vegetation – I think I just saw smoke come out of his ears. Yup, his brain has officially short-circuited.

"Reuben ain't gonna call you *Blanky*," he says, I think a little concerned for one of us in this cell, though I'm not sure who.

Nonetheless, he seems satisfied enough and takes his leave of my room.

Deepvoice still looks broken to me. I was joking before but now I'm really starting to wonder if I've given him a stroke or something. Aside from rumoured broken hips, I really don't know what takes out an old guy, and I sure as hell don't know how to fix it.

"Ain't nobody in this place gonna call you *Blanky*," I hear snarled behind me.

"No such thing as a private conversation in this place, is there?" I shout back at Laz.

"It's no wonder you're so sensitive about it. You sure got the short straw in names, boy," he says back to me.

I chuckle. He has no idea what I call *him*.

"You okay, there, Abe?" I ask.

"You a different boy today, that's for sure. You fall and hit your head someplace?" he asks me. I'm just relieved that he's not broken, at least not irreversibly anyways.

I know that I promised him that I'd tell him the story, but as the Beast has made perfectly clear, everyone's an audience member here.

"It's a long story," I say. "We'll get to it, don't worry."

I hope that's enough for him, at least for tonight.

I finish up my dinner. I can feel the meat sitting heavy in my stomach, but it's a nice feeling. I tuck my bundle down beside the bed leg, and stretch myself out.

I can still see "Bathtub" scrawled across my right wrist. It isn't as vibrant anymore, but it's clear enough. I check my left hand. The contrast in the numbers stands out to me for some reason. The finely inked, perfectly aligned numbers that make up my identity. Underneath are rough swollen numbers, angry red and scabbing, so contrary to how I ever think about the person these numbers belong to. I should be those bloodied tortured marks, not him. And beneath that, in a formal dark blue, almost aligned, with loops in her 2's and top curve in her 5, a little eight year-old kid who writes like any teenage girl I ever went to school with. I'm starting quite a collection apparently. 001014126. 007097112. 005009122. *Hold up!*

09. I keep thinking that she's eight – I don't even know where *that* number came from, probably because she seems so tiny, so innocent and vulnerable. 09. If that's her processing year, she's at least –

05. She'll be ten soon. May 22nd. Either she was born here or processed very early. If I remember correctly, we're still in March. She can't be older than ten or they would have moved her already. She's got two months left. No wonder she's already worried about getting more labels, she's ripening up. She'll be transitioning soon. That's hard to picture, not because I can't imagine it, but because I can. That sweet little girl being led away, stripped down, head shaven, four new pinches; that one at the back of the neck is particularly memorable. I can

already see her crying, scared out of her mind, walking into a new room where everyone towers over her. I think about my friend Marley; sweet girl, but her spells scare even those who have known her the longest. I can't imagine poor little Beth walking into that, her first night filled with screaming violent tantrums, self-mutilations, and no one reacting or trying to help. It didn't seem that traumatising when it happened to me, but I was already fifteen; on top of that, I already had my fair share of traumatic experiences.

Why did I run? If I had just stayed put I could have met her right at the door. I could have showed her the ropes, been someone she could trust in the Freakhouse. I was Blanky after all; wasn't that my job? *Was?* I guess so. I *was* Blanky. *"Ain't nobody in this place gonna call you Blanky."* That may be true down here, but somewhere up there someone still will.

Hang on, Bathtub. I'm gonna make sure D46 takes good care of you.

9

TAKEN

I hear the loud *clank*. It startles me out of a dreamless sleep, or maybe I was dreaming and the sound is the only thing I remember. My eyes are heavy and I can feel that it's not time to get up yet. Maybe someone's being taken away tonight. I brace myself for the panicked shouts that might soon follow. I hear the door move, the hinges grinding in a spine-chilling way. It sounds close, or at least closer. So far all the noises I have ever heard have been rows upon rows away from me. This one could be across the way, or down the other end of my row. With no real walls separating us, sound doesn't exactly get muffled out around here.

"Hey!" I hear shouting really close to my ear. It's Toothless. He's not just shouting, he's banging something on the bars between us.

Not Toothless. Please not Toothless. He's the most harmless guy in this whole place. He's also probably the oldest and most worn down. What could they possibly want him for? What possible use could they have for him?

He's banging the bars over and over again. I open my eyes and see him standing in front of the partition, empty metal bowl in hand.

"Not the boy!" he hollers.

In that exact second I flip over and see that it's *my* door that's open. It's *my* cell that now contains a White Coat and two attendants. I don't know if it's instinct, a spasm, or plain clumsiness, but I roll right onto the floor, feet tangled in thin blankets.

The attendants jump on me, grab my arms and hold me down. I try to kick my feet, but I've managed to get them wound up so good that there's no shaking these blankets off of me without my hands.

Toothless's racket has successfully drawn on more attention. Laz is in front of his partition, making the same noise as ol' Joe, and Abe's hands are violently trying to bring down the partition that's tied on my side of the bars.

"He ain't done nothin'!"

"He's just a kid!"

"Let him alone!"

I don't say a word. I know it won't do any good. I don't know if they're going to make me walk out of here, or if they're going to stick me and drag my unconscious body out. I'd rather walk. I doubt they'll give me the option.

This seems familiar. As the dark uniformed goons push me down into the cold concrete, they move their heads so that I can actually see who's standing at my feet. I'm not the least bit surprised. I don't shout. I sigh.

He clearly sees that I'm not struggling. He doesn't speak to me, he just lifts his hand and gestures me to rise.

The attendants still have quite the death-grip on my arms, but they back up as they pull me to my feet.

"What's up, Doc?" I say, my voice still groggy and quiet from having been fast asleep just a minute ago.

The noise around me stops all at once. I don't know if they're stunned or taking their cues from my calm demeanor. Either way, if the White Coat has anything to say to me, he's sure got himself an audience now.

His icy sunken eyes aren't humored at all – I doubt they've ever been.

"Do I need to have you restrained?"

I'm shocked. He's actually addressing me in front of people; if he would even consider these guys to be *people*.

Between criminal lab rats and minion guards, I doubt Dr. Parish would think of any of them as being personified. He's probably very skilled at blocking that out. Plus he's had years of practice.

"I won't bite," I say cockily.

"One of the least of my worries when it comes to you," he says.

I almost laugh. Are we bantering? Have we become such old friends already?

He signals the attendants and they grudgingly let me go.

"Am I coming back?" I ask.

Parish doesn't reply. I didn't really expect him to.

"Just a second then." There's no point in asking for permission. I don't think Parish cares what I do. He must know that I'm not going to go on a violent rampage. I'm much better at hurting myself than others.

I can tell that the attendants are far more wary of me. They've tensed up even worse now that I'm not under their direct control. I push past them and kneel at my bed side. I'm sure that they think I have a weapon of some sort. The attendants are getting ready to pounce. I get up slowly, my lunch bundle clearly in my clutches. They still don't trust me.

I push past them again. I'm right in front of Abe, Deepvoice, who managed to rip down a corner of the partitioning sheet. I have to realign some of the stuff in it, but I manage to squeeze it through the bars.

"Don't let it go to waste now," I tell him.

He looks so heartbroken.

"You'll come back," he tells me, I think more so to make himself believe it.

I nod – it'll make him feel better.

"I always do," I say.

He clutches the bundle like it will bring him salvation. Maybe for him it will.

"Let's go," I say to Parish with a carefree shrug. I'm sure my aloofness is bothering him more than anything. He'd be used to the fighting, the cursing, the crying. I can't give him that kind of satisfaction.

Parish takes a few steps backwards and then leads the way. The attendants stay determinedly close at my heels as I follow. Down the walkway, around the corner, through the door, up the ramp, to the elevator – the predictable route.

"Missed me, huh?" I say to Parish just before the elevator doors open to let us out.

He isn't amused.

We get to the pristine white hallway that just screams "medical building". I'm pretty sure it isn't his official office, there's no name on the door, and the inside is pretty unremarkable. I lean against the wall and wait for him to get settled. He tells the others to "leave us" and then the door closes.

"Sit," he orders.

I hop up on the patient bed, feet swinging impatiently.

"You think you're clever, don't you?" he says accusingly.

I chuckle. "If I were, do you really think I'd be here right now?"

"You can play naïve but you can't play stupid. You've barely been down there for two weeks and you're roaming the building like you own the place."

"Know about that, do you?"

"Know? You're lucky that I know about it. Intercepted a call made to maintenance concerning the strange noises in the ceiling. Thought we might have rodents. *Very large* rodents. I thought better of it. Thought I'd find out where you could have gotten to. Your little action hero moves need some fine tuning."

"Saw some footage?"

"Saw some little idiot poking his head out in an empty room and go rolling about the floor, yes."

"And figured I'd use some Spiderman skills and climb walls? You sure it wasn't rats?"

He wants to slap me so badly right now, I can taste it.

"We already *have* rats and no one *but* maintenance complains about them."

I've got nothing. I know what I did. I'm not sorry about it. I just want to see what his next move is. I stare at him blankly. The ball's in his court, it's his move, it's always his move.

I think he knows that I'm relinquishing any sense of control over our banter. He takes a few slow breaths. I can see how dramatically his chest expands and then shrinks down again.

"What is it going to take to get you to just stay put?"

I shrug. "I'm easily bored."

Stupid thing to say, I know, but I'm already losing this battle.

He covers his brow with his hand. I'm giving him a headache.

"Despite what you may think, *Dotan Abbott*, I am trying to have your best interest in mind. But you are making this excessively difficult. I shouldn't have to hunt you down every day just to see if you're minding yourself or running off to get yourself killed!"

I've never seen Parish express so much emotion. For all the years that I've known him, for everything that Jos, his son, has told me about him, it isn't like him to care about anything. I guess except his work, which technically I am now. Wherever this is coming from, he certainly has my attention now.

"Legally I have obligations. With you being so troublesome, there are certain policies that I am required to follow. *But*, we have options. What will come to pass is entirely dependent upon you and what you choose to do. I'm willing to consider that you are, somewhere in there, a rational adult. Don't try to make a fool of me, I promise you it will only go all the worse for you."

"*Worse*? How?" I blurt out. "I've been imprisoned, used like a medical experiment, starved, beaten, drugged up, taken away from the one place that ever felt like home to me. Trust me, you can take what you want from me. My blood, my legs, my kidneys, hell, take my freakin' beating heart and just end it! There is *nothing* you can do to me that I can't do worse to myself! Bring it on!"

"Your depression can be treated," he says. It catches me

off-guard. He's got his professional face on. "Your lifestyle improved. I understand that your current situation makes any future prospects seem pointless, but there are cards that I'm holding that no one else here can offer you. The *only* way I can help you, Dotan, is with your compliance. Unlike your previous incompetent physician, I will not jeopardize my career for you, understand that. *But*, I also understand that, for some reason that I may never fully appreciate, you are in fact the one and only thing that my son has ever cared about. I have been a failure in an exceedingly great number of ways. Therefore, if for no other reason, I owe it to him to see you kept safe.

"This place is not *just* filled with tortures. There are ways of living. I don't just mean surviving. I mean ways of thriving within these walls. Opportunities present themselves. Arrangements can be made. It *can* be made an option, even for you, Dotan. But for every wrong turn you take it will take me that much longer to set things in motion."

"So that's your offer? A happy life? Heh, good luck."

"One step at a time. What is it that you need now?"

"Are you trying to bribe me? With what? Food? A better view?"

"You don't seem to care for yourself. You aren't so quick to dismiss others though. Collecting numbers, I see?"

I cover up my wrist. I guess it wasn't realistic to think that he wouldn't notice. Between the bright red glow of my tortured skin and the vibrant blue ink that certainly couldn't have come from the prison ward of Ground Zero, my collection has a spotlight display.

"You have someone in mind, I see. You'd be surprised at what I could do."

I'm sure I would be. But I'm also afraid. He says that he's doing this all for Jos, but Jos wouldn't care about anyone else in here. He came in purely for me. What about when this deal of ours is over? Would the name I give him be marked? Next on his hit list?

I look up at him. I want to see him square in the eye. That skeletal shape of his doesn't exactly have "trust me" written all over it. But if he wanted to do worse, he certainly could have by now. He may never have liked me much, but he could have shown it in so many ways. Like the hospital. I know it was probably his wife that made him do it, but while I was waiting to find out if my mother was going to live, waiting to find out if my step-father was going kill me for what I had done, it was Dr. Parish who joined in the rescue mission. He and Jos sat with me that whole time. He didn't have to. He could have just picked me up and delivered me like a package, he didn't have to let me wait. He didn't have to keep his eye on Paul in that waiting room. Granted I wasn't an inmate back then. I'm hoping that this is the Dr. Parish that's still standing in front of me.

"If I'm compliant, what happens?" I ask.

"I can let you off easy. I'll put a tracker on you, monitor you for a few weeks, and then see how things develop from there."

"A tracking device? You mean to see where I go?"

"Generally that's the purpose behind them, yes."

"You want to catch me in the act?"

"I want to diminish the potential for *'the act'*. I have the feeling that you'll be less inclined when the mystery of the challenge is taken away from you."

"And this is the easy way out? What's the other option?"

"I schedule you for surgery and we see what happens from there. I'm sure there's someone in need of something around here. It is a large hospital, we have a lot of patients and eager researchers.

"I believe your loved ones would prefer it if you returned undamaged. If you follow through, your friend might be able to share in that more peaceful life I was telling you about."

"You'd get them on the good side?"

He nods.

"No Docs? No drugs? No tests?"

"Everyone needs to be medically cared for, to not have it would be foolish. But, yes, the researching will be removed. Generally these people are given more dignified jobs, a decent exchange rate for services, and comfortable apartments within the Institution. Most of the attendants you see are such people who have remained eligible as they transition out of the Beta ward. Some even find opportunities back in the community, not overtly public roles mind you, but an opportunity beyond these walls nonetheless.

"I told you, you would be surprised at what I can do. Should you have a person in mind, I may be able to override the prerequisites, make a few recommendations. If not for yourself, then for someone else? Someone you care about? Someone you would like to see safe and cared for?"

"Just one?" I ask.

"At the moment I don't trust that you could earn enough merit for me to pull the many strings that it will take just to keep *you* out of someone else's hands, let alone a multitude. You see yourself as quite the hero. I'm sure you'd ask me to release the whole lot of you. Open the door and let you run free. It doesn't work like that. I'm not a *'free-spirited'* man. Everything I do is tied to documentation. I told you, I will not sacrifice myself for you. I am not a hero."

"I just have to be tracked for a few weeks and you'll promise me that someone, anyone of my choosing, will be safe and cared for?"

"Are you trying to challenge me?"

"How will I know? How will I know that you don't just ignore them, or turn them in or something?"

"When you check-in, as I will ensure that you do, I will arrange for whatever evidence you need to feel satisfied."

"I want to see her," I say.

"*Her?*"

"There's a girl, she's been sick. If I tell you who she is, I want you to check on her, find a way to make her better. And I want to see her. I want to make sure that she's going to be okay."

I realize that of all the people I could name, there was no reason for me to choose Beth. I guess she just seems so vulnerable to me. She's so tiny, so scared, and she's already in

PARISH

rough shape. If they can't take care of her in such a pampered facility like the kids' ward, how in the hell is she supposed to do better anywhere else? Her first. I'll get her on to a good start. Her clock's ticking faster than anyone else's. Two months. Parish has two months to make good on his word or he won't even be able to imagine the kind of hell I can raise if I put my mind to it.

"If you stay put and out of trouble, and I mean any complaint or suspicion that could possibly be raised against you, I'll take you back up to Beta myself. Not for good, just to check-in. We'll go a week at a time. Fair?"

"No. Not Beta. She's not there."

Parish raises an eyebrow.

"You want her number or not?" I say.

Parish takes up his tablet and taps it to life. He looks up at me when he's ready.

I recite it off of my wrist. 005009122.

He's quite serious as he types it in, then he looks up at me again. "The Care House? You actually interacted with the children?"

Care House? Somehow that doesn't seem like the name I would have picked for the kids' ward.

I ignore the comment.

"Did you get it?"

"Once more," he says.

I repeat the number again and he types in the last couple of digits.

"Elizabeth Cross," he reads aloud. "Is this the girl?"

Beth. But I feel like I know that name. I knew someone who had that name. *Elizabeth Cross.*

"She's been sick. She says it's been for a long time. She transitions soon."

"End of May by the looks of it. As soon as a bed becomes available."

"I don't want her going in sick. She's got enough to worry about."

He scans through a few pages, I can tell by how he's sliding

98

his fingers across the screen.

"She had a fever reported a couple of weeks back. Most recent update states that the fever has cleared but severe coughing remains."

"Severe is right. Thought she was going to turn herself inside out," I say.

"Probably a flu bug of some sort. Recent additions can bring just about anything in with them. It's usually worse with children, and far harder to contain. I'll look into it. I'll coordinate with her physician and arrange to meet with the girl myself. Does that suit you?"

"And you'll let me check-in on her?"

"If it can be arranged."

"A week at a time?"

"If it can be arranged. I can't exactly just put you on a leash and take you for a walk."

"I wouldn't do well on a leash anyways," I say. I don't know if he's getting the same picture I am, but I think that we both know that I wouldn't be the first one to heel when expected to.

"So we are agreed?" he asks.

"I suppose we are."

"Good."

He completely changes his stance. He's done. He's walking out.

"Wait," I say, hopping down and following him. "Don't I get that tracker?"

"Of course," he says. "Dotan, it's 3:30 in the morning. I've had a very long day. Get some sleep. You'll find linens in the cupboard."

"Will I go back?" I ask.

"Back?"

"To Zero?"

"Well I certainly can't keep you up here. Right now it's the only place you're allowed, that is if you wish to remain conscious as I suspect that you do. Good night, Dotan Abbott."

How the hell did I get myself out of this one?

Compared to the so-called bed I sleep in in the prison, this was like sleeping in a heaven made of cotton candy. I was out the second my head hit the pillow. I must have slept deep too.

When I wake up, there is a tray on the desk with a silver cover over it, a huge glass of juice sitting right beside it, and the most mouth-watering aroma. It smells like Sunday brunch on a holiday, back when food wasn't made to have no flavour or texture, where things could be drenched in maple syrup and the delicious grease turned napkins see-through when you wiped your mouth clean. I have no idea if it's for me or not, but I don't see Parish and for as much as I may question his tactics, I can't imagine that he'd torture me like this, it doesn't seem like his style. Then again, he's probably the kind of guy who takes a fine meal for granted and doesn't even taste what he's eaten – wouldn't even notice that the mere smell of it is shooting down glorious yet painful sensations through my body, making my toes curl. Though I wouldn't try to explain that to him either. The only thing I have to compare it to involves his son and my bare body. The analogy probably wouldn't go over well.

I help myself. It's not a plate, it's a platter! I don't even notice the cutlery sitting on the side, wrapped up in a folded cloth napkin, until I've already dug my fingers in several times. It's amazing, and already I know that I'm going to make myself sick over this, but right now it feels so worth it. I don't even care if it's drugged. It probably is. Damn it, let them put me out. I'll sleep happy.

I'm barely breathing in-between bites. I grab the glass, even before I've swallowed my mouthful. It's so acidic, it burns the moment it touches my tongue. I love it. I feel it hit the back of my throat, chilled and powerful. Of course it would be at that moment that Parish walks in.

I had heard his card scan, but I guess my brain was overpowered by the sensations of deliciousness that it didn't have time to process that someone would actually be walking in. I just caught a glimpse of something out of place in my peripheral, turned around just in time to have tried to breathe with my mouth full beyond capacity. Sure enough I cough. If I can be thankful for anything, it's that I reacted quickly enough to be able to catch most of the mashed up juice covered slime in my hands.

Parish just stands there, not looking very impressed but also not very surprised.

I'm stuck. I know that there's a napkin within my reach, but my hands are completely filled. I stand there like an idiot, holding my own pre-chewed food. I can think of only two options, neither of which make me feel very proud as a human being.

Parish breaks our stare-down first and brings me over the waste-basket.

"Thanks," I say sheepishly. Hands now empty, I grab the napkin and try to clean up my mess.

"Glad to see that the Institution hasn't changed you very much these past five years."

Is he making a joke?

"Leave it," he says as I kneel down to the floor to wipe up some splatter. "We'll make this quick."

He doesn't even ask me to sit. He has the device already to go, it's lying behind his tablet, caught between it and him. He pulls it out and tells me to roll up my pant leg.

That's it. It's just a leg bracelet. He straps it on, locks it into place, all of which takes only a second to do. He activates it and checks his tablet for the response. It feels weird. It's like pulling Velcro shoes too tight, but also pressing a thick battery into your leg. Definitely won't be in the air ducts with this digging into me.

"Seems to be in order," he declares.

"And the girl?"

"It's still early. You have my word, I'll look into it."

I've got no choice but to trust him.

He takes a seat behind the desk and ignores me while scrolling through his tablet.

I don't know what I'm supposed to do with myself.

I guess he clues in.

"Finish up here and I'll see that you get back downstairs."

I use the fork this time.

I'm escorted down, not by Parish, but by a couple of attendants he called on. I don't go back to my cell. It's the middle of the day; they push me out into the yard. I find my way from there.

Deepvoice seems to be moving a little slower when I see him in the greenhouse. I don't make a big deal about being back. I quietly ask him what he needs me to do.

Before I can say another word, he grabs me by the shoulders, repeating "Thank goodness," over and over.

"I'm alright," I tell him. I don't know if he can even hear me because he's still going at it.

"You hurt?" he finally asks. Clearly he didn't hear me.

"I'm fine. Let me off with a warning," I tell him, which isn't a lie; there were plenty of warnings involved in my encounter with Parish.

"'bout yesterday?"

I nod briskly and kneel down to get my hands dirty. He takes the hint and gets back on task too.

"You never did explain all what happened," he says. "Got you in plenty of trouble, though?"

I can't hide my tracker forever. Even with a sheet between our cells, I'm sure he'd notice at some point.

"Could be worse," I say, letting him get a glimpse of my new accessory.

"You lucky, boy," he says.

Am I?

10

THE DOC

I've been anxious ever since making that deal with Parish. I haven't heard anything. I don't know if I even trust that he did anything. It's not just wanting to see her that has me this agitated, it's the countdown. I can't track the days down here. I can't even track the hours. All I can do is count the cycles. That's what it is, it isn't clocked time, it's the number of turns you take living the same day over and over again.

"Bathtub" has faded almost entirely off my arm. If I weren't expecting it to be there, I wouldn't even notice the slightly off-colour outlines of the letters. When I'm not sleeping at night, lying in anticipation that I'll be "taken" again, I get fidgety. It makes me feel like I must be in Blue's skin, the way he jittered all the time. Having him with me like this, having him in my head like this, it's overwhelming in those quiet hours. I stain my fingers, nails, and sometimes even my sheets and shirts. I dig his numbers in deep. I go through the scabs and make the numbers stay.

I've been starting on Beth's now too. One number at a time. It's my personal masochistic calendar. It's a bit messy, and it takes more than some explaining when others see it, but that's not the worst part of it; my daily tasks aren't exactly open-wound friendly. Even Laz holds me over a sink, trying to clean me out, wrap me up so I stop picking at it. Makes perfect sense to me during the day. The nights are a whole other world to me. They aren't there with me during those quiet times. I'm not even sure how much *I'm* there during those quiet times.

When my time finally comes, it's earlier on than I expect. I haven't even undone my new bindings yet, though I've definitely been picking at them, pulling out loose strings. It's just Parish this time. He stands in front of my door. I stand square in front of him.

"We'll make this quick?" he says.

I nod. I've been waiting for this. I'm not going to fight. He already knew that though, that's why he's alone.

He opens my cell unceremoniously. I step out, my whole body tense, but I remain silent. I follow him obediently. I wait until we're in the elevator before I bother saying anything.

"Did you see her?"

He leaves me drowning in my own question for what seems like ten or fifteen minutes. Logically it couldn't have been, we were still in the elevator, but even if it was only a few short seconds, they were painful.

"I did."

That's it. That's all he says. We reach our floor and I know that there's no point until we're safe behind another closed door. Fortunately, he doesn't disappoint me. I don't even have to pry it out of him. I sit on the patient bed, he takes his seat, the desk chair already in place nearer the bed.

"Elizabeth Cross has pneumonia. Most likely developed around the time of her fever. She's also an asthmatic. I checked her file. Note was made of it some years back, but apparently was never followed up on. Two respiratory conditions have not made recovery easy. I've prescribed something for her, provided that her pneumonia is not viral, she should already be seeing some improvements. I've already arranged a follow-up. We're scheduled for the morning."

"*We?*"

"That was our arrangement, wasn't it?"

Thank you.

"As for you," he continues, "you've been doing well?"

I shrug... I nod unenthusiastically.

"May I?" he asks. He's looking at my bandaging. Blood-soaked old rags. I'm sure he's already imagining in horror the bacteria breeding ground that's lurking underneath. I hope he has a strong stomach.

I hold out my arm. He isn't the least bit gentle as he undoes the tight knots. He pulls it back and I definitely feel the sting. Some of it has scabbed with the cloth, pulling it has ripped them. I wince and involuntarily make a sharp moaning sound.

He begins a sigh, I can see it rising in him, but he never lets it out.

He folds the cloth over again. "Come with me," he says.

We go out, much further down the hall. I know I'm in for something when I realize that we're in front of a door that actually has his name on it. He swipes his ID card, but it isn't enough. He tabs in a password. Now we can enter.

The lights are already on, dim, but on. As we walk through, the lights automatically brighten. *This* is his office, not just his office, but his life, I can tell. Along the wall is a sofa, but bedding is piled onto it. Clothes are strewn over the backs and arms of the chairs that were supposed to be facing his desk. His desk is three times the size as the one Dr. Isaacs had – a bit tidier, but not by much. Fewer papers and more discarded trays, plates, and paper coffee cups. He's been living here.

Behind the desk is a balcony-like banister that breaks at a central set of steps that lead down to an open floor, at least up to a gigantic set of thick cream coloured drapes that boxes off whatever lies beyond those three steps. That must be his main research lab. I can't see any of it but I can hear the equipment running from here and I'm still pretty much in the doorway.

"Don't touch anything," he says, walking purposefully dead ahead.

I examine the room more. Pictures of his family are up on the wall. Some are from even before I used to live with them. Most, though, are new to me. Jordana, his daughter – boy, I never thought she'd look so grown-up. I guess five years and a couple kids later will do that. Parish has a few pictures of the babies, but not near as many as he has of Jos. There are two professional graduation pictures. Others are of Jos in his medical coat. I guess this was the big ceremony. Jos is either holding impressive looking plaques, shaking hands with important looking old people, or posing with a family member. He isn't smiling in any of them.

It's weird looking at these. It may not have been all that long ago that I last saw Jos in person, but he seems worlds away. Seeing his face here makes me wonder about him, but as terrible as it might sound, I don't miss him.

I turn away and see where Parish has gone to. He's down the steps now, rummaging through the cabinetry.

"Come here," he says. It's like he knew I was finally paying attention, though he never looked up at me.

I do as I'm told.

He has me hold out my arm again, but this time he lets me take off the bandaging. Of course it doesn't hurt as much, the damage has already been done. As if to make up for it, Parish puts a sanitary wipe on me. I don't know if it's the chemicals that hurt or just the cold that pierces to the back of my brainstem. He then pulls out a wrap of his own, probably a more sterile one than what Laz has been using on me. He wraps it firmly and then puts a strong white tape over it. It'll be harder to get this one off, but knowing me, I'll manage.

"Will you let me give you something?" he asks.

Do I have a choice?

"It'll help you sleep."

"I don't need help to do that," I say in a joking tone.

He doesn't buy it.

"What?" I say.

"You're sallow. You're obviously easily agitated. And I know that the environment you're in won't help with your recovery."

"My *recovery?*"

"It will take some time, but yes, you will recover."

From what? Life? The lack thereof?

"I can give it to you for tonight. It will help. We'll discuss the rest tomorrow."

I'm supposed to be compliant, aren't I? I don't exactly agree to it, but I'll do what he says.

He's planned this. He has a small bottle ready. He lets two cylindrical pills tumble out into the cap. He puts them in my hand and then fills up a paper cup from the tap.

"You'll have to go back to the other room," he says to me as I knock back the pills one at a time.

"I'm not surprised," I say. "Looks like you've already got a tenant in here."

I thought I was being clever. Should have known better than to think Parish would get it. I actually had to point out the state of his office, the bedding on his sofa. Clearly he's been here more than he's been home.

"You might not realize how demanding my job is yet, but I'm sure you'll understand soon enough."

Thanks to Jos, I also understand that he and his wife haven't been on the best of terms these past five years. I'm sure that has a part to play in the state of his office too.

He has to escort me back to the empty room. He is exhausted, but he does very well at trying to hide it, better than I'm doing, but then again, maybe that's the drugs kicking in.

He pulls new linens down for me and I manage to arrange them as I would imagine a drunken sloth would do. But it's good enough and I fall face first into my new favourite bed. I don't even remember Parish leaving the room; I think I was already out before he could get that far.

I wake up actually feeling rested. My breakfast tray is already on the desk waiting for me, but this time so is Parish, coffee in hand, reading his tablet.

"Mornin', Doc," I yawn out as I stretch.

My bandaging is still fully intact. For a moment I feel a little proud of myself – then I realize that it really has nothing to do with me so much as being knocked unconscious. I don't dwell on it for too long. I have a hot breakfast waiting for me.

Parish rushes me through this morning. I don't mind. We have a mission today.

He pulls out a laminated badge and pins it onto me. All it shows is my barcode, my numbers, and "Accompanied."

"What's this?"

"It's the board-approved pass that will keep me from being arrested. Isaacs should have considered investing in such things – then again, I doubt he'd be approved for it."

"What makes you say that?"

"I would have denied the request personally."

"Let me guess, you make the final decisions?"

"Hardly. I simply follow the rules."

"And making these deals with me is within the rules?"

"A doctor's job is rooted in flexibility and negotiation as much as it is in procedures. The key is knowing when to do which."

I laugh a little. "Not something I'd be cut out for, then, huh?"

"Not even close," he says so dryly that I *know* he's joking with me now. *That'a boy, Parish!*

We get in the elevator. I feel my throat closing up. I wonder what Beth will think when she sees me walk in with a White Coat. Does she even know what a White Coat is?

Parish and I are met by one of the caregivers. She leads us to a small nurse's room where Beth is already waiting. She's sitting up on the bed – it looks so tall with her tiny legs dangling over the edge. I'm almost afraid that she'll slip right off.

Parish's whole demeanour shifts. The moment he walked into that room, he somehow softened. I've never seen that before, not from him.

"Hello, Elizabeth. Do you remember me?" he greets.

She nods her head.

I can't help myself.

"Hey, Bathtub," I say casually.

The look on her face! She lights right up! She hops down in

a single bound, arms open. I kneel down so that she can reach.

"How you doin', kiddo?"

"You came back!"

She's still coughing. I can hear it rattling at the back of her throat.

Parish clears his throat, cuing me that time is precious.

I pick her up and plop her back onto the bed. Parish scans her number and then proceeds to do a basic check-up, much like Jos did for me – the supervised version I mean.

Beth coughs a few times during the check. It's not near as bad as when I last saw her, but Parish doesn't seem pleased about it. His face twists into knots every time she does it.

She tells him that she's been feeling better, but as she adds to her story it turns out that she still gets tired really quickly when she gets put with the other children. The more she pushes herself, the worse she gets. Her throat is raw from the constant coughing, and she's still rubbing her chest as if it will make the pain go away.

Parish takes a swab of her throat.

"I'll run the sample and see if there's any improvement," he tells me.

I wonder if he'll let me stay for the results. I don't even know how long it takes to get results.

"Do you think there is any improvement?" I ask him quietly.

"I had hoped to see better. It shouldn't take this long for her symptoms to pass now that she's being treated."

I'm not a doctor, I don't know much outside of my high school science classes, and I stopped attending those at fifteen so I'm sure I've missed out on some really basic essential bits of information, but I have a thought nonetheless.

"Doesn't pneumonia happen when you're cold?"

"Correlation not causation," he says robotically.

If that's supposed to answer my question, I guess I really did miss out on some major stuff.

"She sleeps top bunk," I say, pretty much ignoring whatever it is that he said. "She's right beneath the vents. They aren't freezing or anything, but they're still pretty breezy."

He taps away at his tablet. Maybe he's ignoring me back, who knows.

"We've done all we can for today," he says to the caregiver who's been standing awkwardly in the corner. "Until next time, Elizabeth."

I wink at her.

"You're coming back?" she asks me.

"Only if I'm really good," I say to her.

She giggles. "Be good then."

I help her hop down and hand her off to the woman.

In the elevator, Parish asks me how I know where the kid sleeps. The way he says it I know he's already figured it out, but I assure him that I'm not some sort of pedophile.

"I'll talk to her caregivers. We'll see about moving the child. Might be an idea to have her placed in that small room for observation. Temperature seemed normal to me."

I agree.

We're already there. I'm surprised at first, but then I clue in. We didn't go up, we went down, and there's only one stop to go when we go down. Parish asks for my badge back. I hand it over.

"So what's the deal this week?" I ask.

"For now, you sleeping. Continue to stay out of the air ducts, obviously. I'm still working on a discreet way of alerting some of the building caretakers that our screens need to be more securely welded. The last thing we need is for you to have inspired a new set of runaways."

"Hey, I didn't runaway, remember?"

"Perhaps not, but I doubt others would have the same change of heart. In the meantime, I want to give you these." He hands me a small envelope, narrow and only about as tall as the palm of my hand. "No wandering, no cutting, and no distributing or selling."

"*Selling?*"

It's the sleeping pills.

"You don't *have to* take them," he says, "but it may do you better than not, at least for now."

"I don't know, Doc, that's a pretty big to-do list you've got for me there."

"You'll be permitted at my next follow-up if that's what you're wondering."

"Can I visit her?"

He raises an eyebrow.

"I mean actually sit and talk with her, not just look over your shoulder as you stick a thermometer in her ear."

"What *is* your fascination with his child?"

I shrug. I bow my head and shuffle my feet.

"I don't know. I guess… I guess it's just nice to be needed again. That's who I was in D block. I was the guy who made everyone feel better. In Zero – in Zero I'm just some dumb kid who can't even take care of himself. I'm a waste of space. Maybe I always was – pretty sure that you've always thought so.

"Sometimes it's just nice to be around someone who doesn't think you're such a waste, even if they're wrong. It's refreshing, makes it seem like maybe some little part of it was actually worth it."

Parish nods in one slow stroke.

"Perhaps I'll consider it a part of your recovery."

He sounds like it's something he needs quite a bit of time to consider. It was a longshot anyways.

"Till next week then," I say.

He scans the door open. "Next week," he repeats.

I'm glad that Parish gave me the envelope instead of the bottle. Living in a world that is void of pockets does not make carrying things easy. I actually end up slipping the envelop into my shoe, which I'm sure isn't actually the best place to be keeping medication, but really, my options are pretty limited. When I get back to my cell, I find a place to stash it under the blanket I've been using as a bedsheet. It sits in the corner between sheet and mattress.

I tell myself that I won't take them, but it doesn't take long, when everyone else has gone quiet, aside from the snoring, that I start focusing on that left wrist of mine. The bandage is a little less pristine white now, but it's certainly still very secure. I find myself tracing my finger over where the numbers should be. I try to force myself not to do it. I close my eyes, stick my right arm behind my head so that it can't move, but then I'm not comfortable enough to be able to sleep on my back like that and it keeps me up.

I slide the envelope out and drag out just one of the pills. I run my tap and drink from the running stream. Mouth full of water, I drop the pill in and swallow it down. It doesn't hit me right away but I feel like the pressure is off now. I tuck the envelope back into place and curl myself up.

I'll be good.

I quickly discover that we aren't given enough hours of rest when the morning buzzer sounds and I can barely shuffle my feet across the floor. It's not worth it to take the medication every night, so I put it off. The later it gets, the more I realize that I probably should have taken it, but the later it gets, the worse it will be to take them. It's a losing battle either way. It's a good thing that the medical tape has a strong grip. My ceaseless picking is wearing down the life of it.

After a few days of dishes and a much needed trip to the showers, there isn't anything seamless about my bandaging. I'm hardly paying attention when I get most of the tape off. When the end of the bandage is loose and flapping, I realize that I'm in trouble. There's no tying it. I try to tuck it inside the inner layers, but I only manage to loosen the entire thing instead. I spend that night with my arm completely buried inside what I had been using as a pillow. Another pill down, just in case.

I realize in the morning that I'm not taking the drugs to sleep, I'm taking it to distract me. I wonder if Parish thought of that.

I have to give Parish some credit: the man follows through. He comes for me, much like before. I sleep in the small examination room, and wake up to a much anticipated hot breakfast. But this time he takes me to his office, his *room* I suppose, and lets me shower. Having a consistently temperatured shower all to myself almost makes me cry. Not to mention being able to use liquid soap. You just don't realize how much those little things matter until they're taken away from you. I get to dry off in a clean fluffy towel, and not worry about who's going to wash it – down the chute it will go.

When I come out, Parish has put out clothes for me.

"Where'd these come from?" I ask. They're a size too big for me judging by the length of the sleeves and pant legs. They look like they'd fit the Doc. I really don't want to wear *his* clothes.

"My son's. I doubt he'll be asking for them any time soon."

"I can't," I say regretfully, "it wouldn't be right. Besides, I don't think he'd want me to after all the good I've done him."

"The Care House ward has concerns about our little arrangement. I may barely have the board's approval, but that doesn't mean that they won't revoke it at any moment."

"You mean that the *board* wants me to wear Jos's clothes?"

The look he gives me is almost identical to the one I got when orange juice came squirting out of my nose over five years ago. I feel just as stupid.

"They don't want you looking – or smelling – like a grunt worker. This is what I have access to. Josiah's or not, this will have to do."

Grunt worker? Prisoner! Or does that destroy the little fantasy they have about their utopian world benefiting the greater good? I could really let Parish have it, but I know that any delay now will only be taken out on Beth. I don't want to disappoint her.

I change. The clothes are definitely too big, but they also feel cleaner than anything I've had on for the last month, aside from that towel. I'm given back my "Accompanied" badge and I put it on.

Parish walks me through the so-called *"Care House"*. There are a number of concerned looks that come my way whenever we pass by another adult. Parish struts like he's the man in charge. It reminds me of Jos conducting our escape. I guess Jos had to learn it from somewhere.

We walk by a corridor with windows in the doors. Far more friendly than any floor I have yet seen in the whole of the Institution. Inside are the classrooms. We don't stop, and Parish moves at a brisk pace, but from the brief glimpses I get, I can see just as I did from the air ducts.

We move right towards the end of the corridor. There's nothing at the end – nothing of much interest anyways. This is where Parish stops. He stands there, back facing the wall, and watches the empty hall like he's overseeing its effectiveness. I'm just about to ask him what's going on, but as soon as the thought forms I get my answer.

A familiar buzzer sounds. Gently, one at a time, the doors along the hallway are let open. The children aren't allowed to run, but you can see the desire too bottled up inside of them. Some are hopping or skipping while latched onto one another so that they can't move too far too fast. Their instructors – I'm not sure if they are the equivalent of attendants, White Coats, or those caregivers I keep hearing about – try to lead them in an orderly fashion, constantly reminding them to "settle down" if they want to go outside for lunch.

Outside? I'd like to go outside. I imagine that their experience of "outside" is far different than for us in Zero Block. I imagine it looking like recess back in my school days. Who didn't love recess?

I'm getting excited for them. I feel like bouncing and running up and down the hall just thinking about it. For the first time, I'm getting an idea of what Jos must have been thinking when he and his friends used to drop in on our soccer games, crossing the field between the Junior High and the Middle School. Big kid or not, sometimes you just need to run around and play, even if it's with kids you could probably step on.

One of the instructors hangs back, waiting for the crowds to pass. It's not until the corridor clears out a little more that I notice the instructor isn't alone. She's got her hands on the shoulders of a little girl. She's holding Beth back.

My heart sinks. *Not like this.*

When the last child is well beyond them, the instructor leads Beth towards us. I see her face light up. She's bouncing inside too.

I get down on my knee.

The instructor let's go and Beth runs straight towards me.

"Hey, Bathtub," I say after she's rammed herself into my chest like a pro football player.

Her arms are latched tightly around my neck. She's almost choking me, but I won't say anything, I won't even pull her off.

"How're you doing?"

She's all smiles. Sweetest little girl.

"Significant improvements since last you saw her," Parish says from above me.

"No more coughing," Beth says proudly, releasing her grip on me. "And I have this!" She shows me an inhaler that she keeps on a cord around her neck. "I didn't even have to use it once today!"

"That's great!" I say, trying to be just as enthusiastic about it as she is.

Inhalers were common on the outside, but I don't remember anyone in my ward ever having one on hand. I'm worried that she won't be able to keep it. I shoot a look to Parish. I doubt he can guess exactly what I'm thinking, but I just want him to be aware that I've got questions for him that I need to have answered. If she needs it, I won't let them take it away from her.

The instructor opens up a windowless room on the side. She motions for Parish to enter.

"Come, we have less than an hour," he warns me.

I stand, holding Beth's fragile little hand. "She can't go out?"

Parish stares at me for a moment, so does the instructor.

Then they both silently look at each other.

"You wanted to meet with the girl," Parish says slowly, trying to figure me out.

"Can she go outside?" I ask again.

They exchange those looks again. Neither making even an attempt to speak to one another.

"Medically," Parish says, finally interrupting the emptiness, "there's nothing to prevent her."

He's put the ball in the instructor's court. She *must* be a caregiver.

"The other children…"

"Will hardly be bothered by it, I imagine," Parish finishes.

Way to go, Doc! I've never been so proud of him!

The instructor closes the door, a bit loudly and very abruptly. We've successfully managed to piss her off already. I'm sure Parish will lecture me on it later, but right now he's on my side. She marches impatiently down the corridor, following the ghost trails of the other children. I walk with Beth, who is skipping beside me. Parish follows in behind, still on watchtower duty. I half expect him to start warning us of icebergs up ahead! I guess he isn't *that* cool yet, but I'm working on him.

It feels great to be let out into the sunshine. The kids are scattered all over the place in this small playground. A bunch are crowded over top of each other on picnic tables, eating what looks like hotdog lunches with fresh cut vegetables.

Beth looks back at me. I nod and let go of her hand. She runs and gets in line with a plate.

I take a few steps back and just watch.

"She *is* getting better?" I ask Parish as he wanders up from behind me.

"Much. The isolation was successful and she has spent the past three days in a lower bed. She's returned to her usual routine without any complication thus far."

"Thus far," I repeat. "What about two months from now? Do you expect any *complications* then?"

"With or without *your* interference?"

Touché, my friend! "Will it require my interference?"

"Her own anxiety will be her own worst enemy."

"You can do something about that, right?"

"It's not my specialty, and I wouldn't recommend it. I've noticed that you prefer a more conscious state, yourself. I don't imagine that you would wish any different for someone else."

I think of Marlene. When walking around the common areas of the ward you were far more likely to see her bound up, dead to the world, drooling on herself. Maybe that's why it scared people so much to see her actually alive a little. No, I wouldn't wish that on anyone.

"So you do care," I say.

"Surprising, isn't it? It's *not* actually a prerequisite that you discard your humanity when you enter this building, despite popular belief among our patients," he says.

"I guess not. You almost sounded like a real person for a second there."

Beth comes running towards me and drags me to a patch of grass that she and a few other kids have claimed as their circle. I'm immediately put on centre stage. I'm asked hundreds of questions. I try to answer them as comically as possible and they seem to like that better anyways. It also makes it a lot easier to avoid questions that I know they don't really want the answer to. Like, "Where do you live?" I'm not touching that one in any more detail than I can get away with. I also try to eliminate as many references to me popping out of the ceiling as possible, but that gets hard when Beth's honour is on the line. I can't have the others thinking she's crazy. I think that I handle it pretty well.

Our time is so short. Before I know it, the buzzer sounds and the caregivers are rounding all the kids up. No one, not even myself, could account for how much time it was going to take for those kids to get ready and back inside with me out there. The line-up of hugs I had to give out was crazy. I also made the big mistake of picking up Beth and spinning her in the air as a hug. They wouldn't leave me alone until they got a turn – especially the really little ones. Kids I wasn't even talking to ran over to me with their hands in the air. Even I was running a little short on patience, but I couldn't say no. I don't know how many times I said, "last one," only to have some puppy-eyed four year old wander up.

Parish had to save me from it. He took me by the shoulder and led me out, kids waving me goodbye the whole while.

"Who would have guessed that you would have done so much better in the children's ward?" Parish said to me, a joke in his voice.

I was all grins and supressed laughter. *Best day ever!*

"Next week?" I beg optimistically.

He raises an eyebrow that has "unlikely" written all over it.

"Hey, I was *so* good today!" I argued. "How could I have done better?"

"I think they would have preferred it if you didn't interact with every child in their care," he said. He's being factual. I can tell that he isn't angry, or even concerned. I'm getting better at this.

"It didn't hurt the kids any," I say.

"I can't say that it did."

"I'm still in trouble for that, aren't I? Your *board* is gonna be pissed, isn't it?"

"Most likely."

"Is that okay? Can I get away with it?"

"It is a necessity as part of your treatment. It may just have additional effects that were unforeseen."

"My treatment?"

"Your depression."

"Oh. Right. *That.*"

Why do I have to be "depressed"? Am I actually or is this just a catch-all to cover his own ass? Looking down at the state of my wrist, all the numbers clearly visible from my etching them in, I guess that non-depressed people don't do that to themselves nearly as often as I do. As happy as I am right now, even traveling down to Parish's office, I know that it won't last, not all day.

"You need to stop doing that," Parish says, seeing where my attention has shifted to.

"Some days are better than others."

"You're no good to anyone if you get a blood infection. In your current living conditions, it could kill you if left untreated."

"So change my conditions!"

He sighs, shaking his head.

"You put yourself in there, remember?"

I sigh too and then go and change back into my disgustingly grubby everyday wear. I feel dirty just slipping into them again.

When I come out and ask Parish what my next task is for this week, he just hands me a felt marker.

"What's this for?" I say, taking it from him. It's permanent.

"You can mark your body up however it is you see fit. Just don't cut yourself," he orders.

I can't make any promises. It isn't just the numbers. There's something else to it. It's the motions of it. It's the pinch and the sting. It's the numbness. It's looking at it and being disgusted, being hateful, being scared. It's after the fact, knowing that I've done wrong, knowing that I'm only making it worse, knowing that others are judging me for it. I both love and hate the shame that comes with it. I can't let go that easily, but I try to humour him.

Standing right in front of him, I begin to write over top of my fresh new bandaging. I put down three numbers: mine, Blue's, and Beth's.

I try to hand the pen back to him, but he says, "Keep it."

I just turn towards the door, waiting for him to let me out, when I notice that he isn't coming. He's frozen.

"Is everything – " I begin, but he hushes me and orders me to stay where I am.

He's reacting to his equipment, but I've always heard it making some noise or other so I wouldn't have been able to guess that there was any change in it.

He has already run down to those closed drapes and disappeared behind them.

I listen. I hear it. It's a person. Someone's in pain. *He's had a person in here this whole time?* I feel chills going all through my body. *He's been sleeping in here with a person?* I'm looking frantically around the room. I know there isn't, but I half expect to suddenly notice vials of human parts hanging on the walls. There isn't anything like that, just pictures. Lots of pictures. My brain suddenly makes a connection. The discarded clothes I just had on – Jos's. The walls are covered in pictures of Jos. Parish said from our first encounter that he's keeping an eye on me because of Jos. It's my fault that Jos got in trouble, got caught, quit the county all together – or maybe he didn't.

I am genuinely freaked out. I have no way out on my own. I don't think that I could go without knowing – without knowing for sure.

I ignore what Parish said to me. I make my way one step at a time as quietly as ever, knowing that if I even get a glimpse of what is behind that curtain that I've probably sealed my fate once and for all. But I need to know. I need to know what Parish is hiding. I need to see if it is Jos back there. I need to know if Parish is so sick and obsessive that he'll do whatever it takes to keep his son with him, in Lantham, in the Institution. I want to throw up and I'm not even close enough yet to see anything.

The disturbed moaning is louder. He's sobbing. Parish is speaking to him in a low whispering voice. I'm so concentrated on seeing that I can't put the words I'm hearing together. I think there's an, "it's alright, son," in there, but I'm aware that my brain might be making that up.

The drapes are open just enough that I can see the patient bed. Feet covered in blankets. I can see a few of the machines in the background and Parish going back and forth. I reach my hand out. I'm barely touching it, but I push the curtain to the side just enough to give me a better view – even though my heart is in the back of my throat, ready for me to spew it out at any moment. I don't. In an instant it drops out of my throat and hits the bottom of my toes in a thud so loud that I'm surprised the whole building isn't echoing it back to me.

"Zac?"

"I TOLD YOU TO STAY BACK THERE!" Parish screams at me.

I'd push my way right through the Doc if he tried to stop me. I go straight to him, afraid to touch him, fearing that he could dissolve at any slight contact. He can't be real. It can't be him. It's a dream. It's a hallucination. It's a fake. A clone. It's something that isn't right. It's something made just to hurt me. It's killing me because I want it to be him more than anything.

I can't breathe. I can't see. My hands are digging into the blankets around him. I'm shaking uncontrollably. I can barely hold myself up. I can't stand. My knees are mush.

I burry my face in the blankets at his side. It clears away a little bit of the endless waves pouring down my face. His eyes aren't open. There are tubes all around him. His colourless face is contorted, the same tension as when he used to –

Parish orders me to get out of the way. He's rapidly trying to get the tubing out of his throat as his strapped down body convulses.

"Hold his head!" he orders. I guess he realized that I wasn't going anywhere.

He gets the tube out. It's so long that I can feel him pulling it out of my own stomach.

"The straps!"

I pull the blanket down and see he's strapped in much the same way I was when I was prone to violent spells. Between the two of us we get them off relatively quickly, given that we are both trying to keep him secure at the same time. Parish turns him over onto his side and lets the fluid spurt out of his mouth. I remember holding him myself only too well. I keep a hand on his head, his once head of thick fluffy blond-grey hair is now gone, shaven down and I can see the red scars at the back of his head where he must have been opened up and stitched back together. I rest my head down on his, going along for the rough ride as we both wait for his spell to come to an end.

I don't even notice that Parish has stuck him until I feel his body start to calm. It's a slow decrease, but then he eases back into a deep sleep. I kiss his head and reach down for his hand. It still feels the same. It still fits the same, even with the tubes and cords.

I can't move anymore. I can't speak. I can't even cry audibly. I am a lifeless mass draped over the only person I have ever loved, waiting for his off-colour grey-blue body to merge in with mine. I want to disappear into him. I want to give him my body, my life, and melt away.

I can hear Parish strapping him back in. When I'm in the way, he tries to move me.

He's surprisingly delicate about it. He gently touches my shoulders, not grabbing me, just cuing me to get up.

"Let's go, son. He's stable now. He'll be alright."

I shake my head violently. "No," I mutter. The saliva in my mouth is so thick that I can barely swallow it. Just saying that one little word has me drooling down the sides of my mouth. I squeeze his hand all the tighter.

"Dotan, we both know that you can't stay here. You shouldn't have seen this. You weren't ready."

I nuzzle my face all the closer to his.

"I won't leave him," I barely say with any clarity.

"He isn't even conscious. He hasn't been for more than a minute at the most."

"I don't care. I won't leave him. I promised him."

I can't see again. The flood washes over my face. I can't breathe.

"I can't keep you here, I'm sorry," Parish says. He actually sounds regretful, even in the state I'm in I can hear that in his voice.

"You can't send me down either," I tell him after sniffling back some of what's choking me. "You know I know how to get out. Nothing you do can keep me down there. You know I'll get out. And I won't just get out. I'll set off the alarms, I'll send people through the tunnels, and everyone will know who to blame for it."

"Dotan," he says calmly, "throwing around threats won't help anyone. I want him to get better. I'm trying to help him get better. If you want that too, you need to help me."

I'm ready. He can ask me anything. I'm ready to do it.

"I need you to go back down. I need everything to continue on. I need you not to worry about this."

I'm sure it sounds like a very logical demand in his head, but this isn't anything to do with him! This isn't his Blue! I kiss his head possessively.

Parish tries to lead me away again, gently. It doesn't work.

"How the hell am I *not* supposed to worry about this! He was dead! He was dead because of me! I have been tearing myself apart and *you've* had him here, *ALIVE*, the whole time!"

Parish tries to calm me, but I won't have any of it. Whatever he says, whatever he offers, I'm not leaving. Let him knock me out and drag my ass back to Zero Block. I'll be right back up here within the hour, alarms blazing!

Eventually, Parish backs off.

"If you're up here, I can't call in my support staff," he says. "It wouldn't look right. You shouldn't even be in here in the first place. If you stay, it's just us in here."

I nod. I understand.

"Let's clean him up a little, wouldn't you say?"

I nod. Reluctantly, I abandon my post and help the Doc. I wipe up Blue's face as carefully as possible as Parish holds his head, not nearly as delicately as I would have liked him to. Once we get him cleaned up, I'm set on cleaning up the small pool in his bed sheets. I've done this so many times before, I don't need Parish to walk me through it, though he still seems to think I do. I dab it up, and while it isn't perfect, it's a vast improvement.

We can't move him with just the two of us. If Blue wasn't so plugged in, we could, but Parish isn't strong enough to manage it delicately and I'm not much better – though the Doc is more concerned about my not being "qualified". Since we can't change out the sheet, we fold up a towel and place it over top of the wet spot. It isn't a perfect solution, and the sheet will need to be changed out soon anyways, but at least it keeps Blue's face out of the wet.

I move Blue's arm very carefully and make a very conscious note of what's plugged in where. I have to undo a few straps in order to pull it off, but I do it quietly so Parish doesn't even notice what I'm up to. I think he's too busy trying to figure out how to explain it when I don't get put back into my cell tonight – or how to carry me back down into it successfully. Whatever it is that he's doing, he can keep doing it. I make sure that Blue has all of the blanket covering him, that none of his parts are being squished or turned in an awkward way. When I'm positive that I can do it without hurting him, I crawl up and lay on my side beside him. I keep his bare head close to me and hold his hand on my stomach. I kiss his face and watch him breathe. It means so much just to see him breathe. I close my eyes, drown out the sound of the machines surrounding me, and just listen for him.

"I'm right here," I whisper to him. "I'm right here."

11

SOMETHING TO LIVE FOR

Parish lets me stay just the one night and not even for all of it. He wakes me up ridiculously early, too early for my brain to process what's going on. He lowers the bed rail and helps me down. He walks me back down to Zero Block. I don't fight it. Blue's alive. Parish has been keeping Blue alive. I may be a child most of the time, but even in my sleepy state I know what's possible and what isn't. The likelihood of Blue surviving was next to nothing. I don't believe that Jos lied to me. I honestly think that he was completely one-hundred percent certain that Blue was irreversibly dead. I've been playing against all of the odds and I'm starting to realize how much Parish has been responsible for that. I don't fight him. I don't even ask him when I can see Blue again. He's earned my trust now. He has done more than enough. When we get to the cellblock, I can see that only a few people have begun to stir for the morning. Parish leads me right up to my cell door to let me in, even if the buzzer is going to sound in an hour or so.

"Thank you," I whisper to him.

"Until next week," he whispers back to me as I get locked back in.

From then on I'm quiet, not sullenly so, but for the first time maybe ever, I'm at peace. I don't make much conversation, but I don't avoid it either. I'm not happy exactly, but in some ways, content. This, of course, has my friends far more worried than anything.

Friends? Yeah, I guess they are. I don't know what to tell them either. They've been curious from the beginning that I have such frequent trips away; they've never seen anything like it. Then again, they've never seen anything like me down here with them either. I come with a whole new set of rules.

"Every time you come back, you's a bit different," Deepvoice says to me.

I shrug, a smile on my face. I can only describe it in Parish's words. "Just treating the depression," I respond. "I think it might be starting to work."

Deepvoice lets out a slow starting belly laugh. "Sure, boy. All the aches and pains we deal with and you gets yourself a therapist. What a world we live in!"

I'm glad he isn't bitter about it. I'm glad that I'm not bitter about it either. The hard long day, the quick cheap food, the absence of toilet paper, I'm doing better with it all. I don't carve at night either. I'll recite Blue's number a few times, but then I get to thinking about something else. Mainly I get caught up in what I'm going to do when Blue ever wakes up again. I've got a list made up in my head a mile long. The one that keeps repeating in my head is his name. Jos recited it to me – seems like forever ago now. His real full name. I don't even know if Blue knows it or remembers it. Zacchaeus Louis Shepherd. It's my new mantra. This is what I drift off to sleep saying to myself.

The spring is quickly blooming into summer. The warm weather has us out of the greenhouse for fieldwork. Every available hand is out readying the farmlands for new crops. It's hard work and completely brutal being under the sun all day, but I know all of that heat would boil us alive in the greenhouse. I feel bad for those who have to go back.

Deepvoice is one of them. They keep me on in the field. I'm pretty much the plough horse for five long rows at a time, then I get to switch off with someone else. It actually hurts the base of my neck more than anything, pushing that wooden thing up and down the field. The guys are as good about it as they can be. A few of them run me water every ten minutes or so. I need it. It's hard to believe that it's only April. I can't imagine how much this is going to kill us in August. I've never known Lantham for being this hot this early when I used to live on the outside – then again, during this time I would be in school and not working a field for ten hours.

I'm sitting on the side, drinking my twelfth bowl of water, watching someone else take over for me. I've soaked my shirt in water and wrapped it on my head. The water is still trickling down my back. I close my eyes to feel it. A breeze rises up and sends a chill through me. It feels painfully good.

I open my eyes only when I think I hear someone saying my name. It's not being called-out, but someone is definitely saying it. I may have been more freely letting others know it, but it's still not something that I hear very often. It's certainly not a name that anyone else has in here. I listen for it again and try to scan my surroundings for who might be saying it. There are so many of us, and most of the guys are gathered in small groups chatting away; it could be any of them.

Way off of the field I see the dark uniforms of the attendants. While we do get attendants out here, they very rarely interact with us without us loading produce out in front of them. There's nothing out here for them right now, and unless there's a serious fight going on, only one of which I have ever seen since I've been here, there's no reason for them to be watching over our work.

Someone points over to my general direction. *Uh oh.* I don't make a fuss about it. I stay where I am and wait to see what happens. If they want me, they'll either come to where I am or call me over. I take another drink and just watch. All of them are looking at me now.

Now I'm being called over. One of the guys has his hands

cupped around his mouth, shouting my name.

I have no choice. I take one last drink out of the bowl and make my way over.

I'm about to ask what's going on when one of the attendants grabs my hand and scans it on a small hand-sized tablet.

"Come with us," they command.

I'm completely obedient, but I guess they weren't expecting that. They grab me roughly, hold my hands behind my back and put a zip tie on me. I don't even make a sound as they do it. The whole thing is needless; they especially don't need to make it *that* tight. I let them. It's just easier to find out what this is all about than to react rashly out here. Even a few of the guys around me are looking like they want to jump in with how roughly I'm being handled. I just stay calm about it and they stand their ground.

"See you in a bit," I tell them casually.

I let the attendants push me back towards the main building. I'm flipping through recent memories, trying to figure out what mess I've gotten myself into now.

Nothing is coming to mind. I've kept my tracker unharmed, I've never even entered the pantry again since my little adventure, I've even been fairly pleasant lately. That being said, I've certainly left a long enough record of up-to-no-good that just about anything could have been thrown under the microscope to determine my punishment... again. And I thought Parish said that there was nowhere worse to put me in this place. Maybe they've only just finished building the worst place, named in my honour. Just for the sake of it, I kind of hope so, just to stay that it happened.

The route we take is familiar enough to me. Up the service elevator, up a few ramps, down a few corners. They're taking me to Parish's office. I've never been brought here without the Doc before. I'm getting a little worried. I hope he's okay. The last thing I need is for him to go the same way as Isaacs.

I'm hoping and praying as they knock on the door. That part throws me off too. I've never seen attendants needing to knock at anything before. Generally they just scan themselves into wherever it is they want go. Forget rogue inmates, I'm surprised that the Institution hasn't gone into lockdown from a scan-happy attendant. I'm sure that they don't get paid enough for this job anyways.

The door opens just an inch, that's all. One attendant grabs it and opens it the rest of the way while the other one pushes me in as if I were resisting, causing me to almost trip over my feet on more than one occasion. Dr. Parish is leaning against the wall, standing very still as he waits for the attendants to finish throwing me around.

"That'll do," he says coldly. He gives a nod and holds the door open for the attendants to let themselves out. It isn't until the door is firmly shut once again that Parish even looks at me.

"I apologize for their conduct. I would have gone myself if it were at all possible."

"You? Out in the middle of a field of free-running criminals? Ha! I'd like to see that!"

"Criminals, yes," he says calmly as he cuts the zip tie. Those guys didn't give him much room to work with so I definitely feel that cold steel pressed into my skin before I'm free again. "Hardly dangerous ones, I'd imagine. Most of them are computer hackers or conmen. Did you think that you were really thrown down with a pack of murderers?" He's the one laughing now, well at least as much laughing as I've ever seen out of him.

"Are you serious?" I feel so let down. "If that's how you treat the harmless ones, what *do* you do with the crazy ones?"

"The Zero Block is filled with imports from outside of Lantham. We don't have a very extensive population, Dotan. Where would we ever come up with hundreds of cut-throat criminals? People know how to handle the extremes, and that's about all. Give someone grey matter and they'll never decide what to do with it."

"A life-sentence seems a little much for an 'I-don't-know-what-to-do-about-it kind of case,'" I say.

"And yet it's what we're built on, isn't it? Just take a look at yourself."

"*Orphans and criminals*," I recite from memories of my old school lessons.

"People *want* to know what happens to the killers and rapists. Those who have no one else in the world to care about what happens to them, well it doesn't take much to convince someone to take them off of government funding."

"Wait. The rest of the country pays to keep criminals?" I ask. My lessons have never really extended beyond Lantham. I'm actually surprised that Parish knows anything about it. "Boy, I'd hate to be locked in one of those places. How long before they resort to cannibalism there?"

Parish almost laughs again as he puts the scissors back in his cluttered desk.

"That's what makes Lantham Institution so ingenious: you cover our costs for us. I'm afraid you might like the other place a little bit better."

I always knew that I hated living on this side of the economic solution. What a crap solution!

"Is this why you called me up? To test out my depression threshold?" I ask.

Parish smiles. "Not as such," he says. "But since you ask."

He doesn't tell me anything. He just tells me to wash up a bit.

I turn around and head for his bathroom. I take my shirt off of my head and give myself a mini-shower in the sink. I can see all of the water stream down the drain as mud. I use the hand soap all up my arms, around my neck, and a bit on my face. I'm trying to go quickly because I know that he's got good news for me. I feel guilty about the pools of water I have let splash all over the floor, but I tell myself that I'll come back and clean it up for him.

I leave my shirt behind. Not only is it completely filthy, but it'll remind me to come back and deal with the lake I created on his floor.

I come out to find Parish already down in the lab.

I have to brace myself to look beyond the curtain this time.

I tell myself that Parish wouldn't have called me up like that if it were bad; I'd like to believe that he would have come himself for that.

Parish pops back out. "It's alright," he says. He's in a good mood. That worries me too. What if *he* doesn't want to see me? I wouldn't want to see me.

Parish pulls the curtains back, opening them up wide.

Blue's laying there, his bed propped up just the slightest bit. He has far fewer tubes in him. Nothing is on his face at all. He looks like he's sleeping.

"He's doing better?" I ask, holding my breath.

"Drowsy, but otherwise better than I could have expected. If I may be so vain, I must say that I have truly outdone myself."

As surprising as it seems, Parish really isn't the kind of guy to gloat, and I never really realized it until he said that. It is so off for him to say anything like that. Elitist? Definitely. Gloater? That's just funny.

"He's been in and out for most of today. I thought you would want to be here."

How could "thank you" ever be enough? I inch my way over. He looks more peaceful now than the last time I was in. What was that? Five days ago? He even has a little more colour to him, at least for what Blue's skin tone allows him to have. Even at his most lively he usually looked a little washed-out. Even so, it never stopped me from thinking that he was the most beautiful thing I've ever seen. Even now, his hair gone, his face thin, he's all I have ever wanted.

I touch his hand softly. It's still hard to believe that he's real. I bend over so that I don't move him too much. I kiss his hand, feel the length of his fingers along my lips, the taste of his fingertips just slightly on the end of my tongue as I kiss them.

I hear him moan and feel him shift. His eyes are still closed but he's sleeping on his own, no sedation. I think he can feel me. I put his hand down and trace his face with the back of my thumb.

"He looks better," I tell Parish. "A lot better."

"You seem to have that strange effect on people."

What? "Me?"

"Compassion can often do what medicine can't. It's certainly not my field, but I have seen it once or twice. It's harder to practice than you might think, especially successfully."

"No," I tell him, "it's easier than you think, it just takes practice. Jos taught me that."

"It wouldn't surprise me if it were you who had taught him. I'm afraid there wasn't much of it to be seen in our house."

"More than you know. You just have to know how to look for it," I say.

"I have tried," Parish says dejectedly, "obsessively, really. Do you know why I came back to Lantham?" he asks me, apparently lost in thought.

"I never knew that you left," I confess.

"Oh yes. I was born in this community, back when they still called it Lanthamville. My story was quite similar to yours, you might be surprised to know, except it wasn't a step-father in my case. He was my biological father. A heavy drinker, but never more so than when my mother died in childbirth. She left me and my young sister. I never did find out if the baby ever survived. He never brought it home in any case.

"We didn't last more than a week in his care. I don't remember how it started, or if there even was anything that started at all. I only remember Teresa. My sister was barely three years old and he was coming for her. I threw myself in front of him, nine years old and ready to take him on single-handedly. I later woke up in a hospital, told that I was lucky to be alive."

He rolls up his sleeve and takes off his watch. It couldn't be plainer, more faded than mine, but as easily readable as any. 006074116. "I was registered and then fostered out almost immediately. It was a rare case indeed for a fostering to take place with an older child, being nine years old at the time, but they took three of us that year, and I was the youngest among them. Their hope was to save us before we became ineligible, hoping that others would follow suit to save the rest. Few did. My sister never made it out.

"My adoptive parents were quite the radicals of their time; they protested against the Institution like no other, nearly risking their lives too. They had no choice but to flee. But I came back. I knew that I had to find my sister one way or another. The Institution openly welcomes professionals, and once I had enough credentials to my name, being hired on was easy enough."

"Did you find her?" I can't help ask.

"I did, but not as I had hoped. I had to apprentice for years, despite my experience, before I was given a private practice of my own. It wasn't as easy as Josiah must have made it look when he used my passcodes. I had to be patient. But I got distracted as well. Between trying to build up my reputation and becoming a new husband, soon a new father, I almost forgot what I was looking for. When my daughter was born, I couldn't forget any longer.

"I found her. Some days I wish I hadn't. She had not been well used. Based on her records, her existence had been quite the horrific one. The Institution did not have the regulations we have in place nowadays. You have questioned how anyone can practice on human beings as we do; well, I can tell you, I certainly questioned how it was done back then. By the time I found her she was deformed and more-or-less lobotomised. This is what the Institution used to be, a complete madhouse. She could barely speak, there was no reasoning with her, and she existed almost entirely bound or tranquilized. I wouldn't have recognized her, nor do I think she ever recognized me, not that I lingered on making any deep connection with her. I did the only humane thing that was within my power at the time – I euthanized her. She went peacefully, out of pain. It was the only thing I could do for her, well, to help her leastways.

"She had left a legacy behind her. A child. Locating him was easy once I had my sister's records. I thought the solution would be simple; I would convince my wife that we needed to sign the foster forms and we would take my nephew and be rid of this place once and for all."

"Why didn't you? Your wife would have done it. I know she would have. She tried to foster *me* for crying out loud!"

"Yes, she would have, and if I would have told her, she wouldn't have let me do any less."

"You didn't tell her?"

"How could I? For what my sister was subjected to, for how much she was altered and destroyed, the child did not go unaffected. The Institution contains all of her records, it contains all of the labeled samples of every experiment ever conducted within its laboratories. For all that the child could carry, for all the signs of what the child did carry, I could not with a clear conscious remove him from the only place that could keep him alive. This has been my life's work, and unfortunately, it has come at the expense of my own family. And yet, right here in the middle of it, is you, all over again. I don't know what it is about you, Dotan Abbott, but for some reason or another our paths continue to cross."

What does this have to do with me? Then I see he hasn't been looking at me at all. This whole time he's been staring at Blue. Zacchaeus Louis Shepherd. "Teresa Shepherd," I say, recalling the list Jos read to me.

"Parish is my adoptive name. I was glad not to be associated with my father - as I'm sure Josiah would be glad to be rid of me as well. Funny how we pass these things on, our worst fears, how they slip through our fingers the tighter we think we've held onto them."

"Zac is your…"

"My responsibility. The only one I have left, I'm afraid."

"Hey," I say, "you're stuck with me, too, you know?"

"So it seems."

Slowly we both start to laugh pathetically. What sad lives we lead, but apparently we lead them within mere steps of one another, twisting and turning on the exact same dance just on different beats.

Parish orders up dinner for the both of us. I hop in the shower and change into Jos's clothes, and clean up the puddles, too. We eat while keeping watch over Blue as he sleeps. He stirs every now and then, but it doesn't even last long enough to get to his bedside.

I crawl in beside him. I don't think Parish particularly likes it but he doesn't say anything against it. If anything, it's giving him a bit of a break. I see him stretch out on his sofa. I lean my head against Blue's. It feels better to have him close to me. I rest my lips on his head and close my eyes.

12

WHOLE

I yawn and start to wake, not feeling rested. I didn't plan on actually falling asleep. I kiss Blue's head and notice that our hands are intertwined. I don't know if I did that or he did. I kiss him again. I very carefully untangle myself and crawl out. I creep quietly back up the steps towards the bathroom, passing by the snoring doctor. On my way I catch a glimpse of the time. It's late. I know that I have to get back down to my cell but I wait until I've used the toilet paper before bothering to wake up Parish.

He jolts as I gently shake him.

"Past my curfew, Doc," I whisper to him.

He wipes his eyes and searches for his glasses on the floor. I lean over and pull them off of his head.

"Thank you," he says groggily. "Anything?"

I shake my head. "Just sleepin'."

"Would you rather stay?" he asks me.

"Are you serious?"

Parish stretches out. "I don't particularly want to crawl in there with him. I *do* have other work to attend to in the morning."

He doesn't have to ask me twice. I say goodnight and leap

down the steps. Even squished up to the side in this patient bed is far more comfortable than anything that's waiting for me downstairs.

"Don't wake up without me," I tell Blue before kissing his forehead. I link our hands and nestle in nice and close.

During the night I feel Blue jolt, it's not a seizure, just a jolt. I hold him all the closer, hush him as he unconsciously moans. It might be interrupting my own sleep, but I'm glad that I'm here.

Morning comes too early. Parish never woke me. And though I can't see any type of clock from the patient bed, I'm positive that it's long after wake-up call in Zero Block. The Doc is up. I can hear the shower running from here. I stretch very carefully and then roll out. For all that Parish has done, and letting me skip out on yard work, I decide to help him tidy a bit. Obviously there's only so much I can do given the disastrous nature of his living space, but I can at least collect all the used dishes and load them up on the tray, ready to have them taken away. I'm actually quite surprised at my skill; I haven't even broken anything yet.

I can't help it, as I'm up on the upper-floor, I keep looking at those pictures of Jos. All of this time he and Blue were cousins. I don't see any resemblance between them. Then again, I don't even know how much Parish and his sister looked alike. There aren't a whole lot of similarities between Jos and his sister; then again, maybe it's because I know how different they are as people, or were back when I actually knew them as people.

I guess I startled Parish. He didn't expect to see me up as he came out of the bathroom.

"Sorry."

At least he had a towel around his waist. I jump in the bathroom now that it's free. I ask him through the closed door why he doesn't just up-grade to one of those apartments he told me about. I'm sure that they would let him have one.

Aside from his illegal activities, he has been quite the contributor to the Institution, you'd think they'd bow down before him by now. At least they could give him a futon.

He doesn't reply to me. Either he can't hear me, or he wishes he couldn't. I don't blame him either way.

I come out to find Parish in hiding somewhere. It doesn't take me a minute to see him behind the hardly closed drapes. He's checking up on his patient.

I need to ask the Doc what his plans for me are. It might seem like a small thing, but if I'm going back downstairs, I really need to change, and I really don't want to. Jos's clothes may have me tripping over my pant legs, but at least they aren't caked in anything unidentifiable.

I get nearer, ready to begin asking my questions, then I hear it.

"How are you feeling?"

At first I think he's asking me, but he's speaking very softly.

"Doc?" I mutter.

"Would you like some water?"

I'm holding my breath again.

"Will you get us some water?"

I nearly fall over backwards, but I comply. I grab one of those little paper cups and fill it at the lab sink. My hands are shaking as I bring it towards the curtains.

There he is, eyes open. Parish thanks me and begins raising Blue's bed just a little bit more. I bring the cup over. Parish takes it. His hands are much steadier than mine. Blue spits up the first sip. It dribbles down his chin and onto his chest. He gets the hang of it though. Parish is doing really well with him. I'm afraid to come closer.

He's trying to move. He's aching all over. I remember what that felt like. Being bedridden for too long has that effect, not to mention a near-death experience. *Near-death?* Who am I kidding? He did die. But he's back. That's all that matters.

Tears well up in my eyes. He's looking right at me.

"Hey," I say. The floodgates open. I'm grinning like an idiot, half laughing, tears pouring down my face like a faucet.

"Hey," he says hoarsely. He holds out his hand towards me. I take it and crumble right at his side.

"I'm right here," I say over and over again, kissing his hand.

"D-id-n't thin-k you c-ould get ri-d of me th-at ea-sy, d-id you?" He's trying so hard to smile.

I cup his face, get right nose-to-nose with him, "Never getting rid of you," I tell him.

I kiss his forehead, his brow, his nose, his lips.

He's staring at me with a puzzled look on his face.

"Sorry," I say. "I was just so scared that I'd never see you again. I've been going out of my mind without you. I am so, so sorry for everything. But I promise you, I'm going take good care of you. I promise."

"Blanky…"

I don't even let him start, let alone finish. I grab him again and kiss him so hard. I feel him tense up from under me. He's shaking a little. I get that this might be a little overwhelming for him – this is after all the most conscious he has been in months – but if I don't do it now, who knows if I'll ever get another chance.

I pull away to let him breathe. He's frozen in place, wide-eyed.

"I missed something, didn't I?" he finally says slowly.

"More than you know," I tell him, a huge smile on my face.

"Catch me up again?" He's so weak, but I see that grin of his trying to shine through.

"You know it," I say. I'm on him in an instant. He's never had me kiss him before, not like this, and I'm pretty sure he's never been kissed by anyone else either. He's loosening up, following my lead. I go slow with him. My hope is that he'll be around for further exploration later, at least when he can sit up on his own accord.

"Are you quite done?" Parish asks, his back turned from us. I laugh.

"Just saying *'hi'*."

Parish turns back around.

"Dotan, I'll need my support staff," he tells me. "I'm sorry,

139

but – "

"You don't have to explain. You let me be here. I'll do whatever, you know that. Just take good care of him."

"If you can't go down, I'll open up the room at the end of the hall."

"If you need me to go down, I'll go."

"I'll get you breakfast first," the Doc promises.

"Wouldn't be the first time I've gone without," I tell him.

"I'll get you something." He looks down at Blue. "You won't be on solids for a while. Are you feeling hungry at all?"

"Starved," he says eagerly, even if it's hoarse.

I get a few more minutes with Blue before attendants are supposed to arrive for me. Parish walks me down to the examination room and I wait there to be picked up. I'm supposed to be brought breakfast. I guess they don't put as much effort in when Parish isn't watching. Then again, one untoasted bagel is still better than nothing. I eat half of it on the way down and hold onto the rest as I get kicked out into the yard. I go to the greenhouse for a starting point. It's stuffy and smells worse than ever, but I couldn't be happier.

Parish makes it up to me. I get pulled out the minute that the cells are locked for the night. The moment I spot the attendants coming down my row, I stand with my back to the cell door, hands behind me, ready to go. It doesn't stop them from handling me roughly, but I'm practically skipping out.

"Couldn't keep me away?" I joke as Parish cuts me out of my bindings.

"Couldn't keep *him* still. He can barely sit up and I've already caught him four times trying to make it towards the door," he tells me.

I'm beaming. *Good ol' Blue!*

"You gonna be able to explain this to the board?" I ask, purposely being cheeky about it.

"Hardly."

I laugh. "I'm sure you'll think of something."

I go down to see him. I'm gross in my prison clothes, but I

need him to know that I'm here.

He's surprisingly alert. He squirms up as best as he can, trying to sit up on his own.

"Hey, Sicky" I say, heading towards his out-reached hand.

Laces his fingers through mine.

"Wondered if you'd come back," he says, his voice still strained.

"Always."

I lean in to kiss his cheek. He nuzzles into me.

"You smell like shit," he says.

I can't help but laugh. "Yeah, I know."

He pulls me back in and kisses me anyways.

"I'll be back," I tell him, handing his hands back to him.

"Where're you going?" he asks, filled with such concern.

I laugh. "Just to the shower. Gonna get this shit off of me. Wanna come?"

I should have known. Blue doesn't skip a beat. He tosses the blanket off of him and grabs the bed rails.

"No! There'll be none of that!" Parish shouts from his desk, doing everything he can not to watch us.

I wouldn't have let him anyways. Hell if I would be able to keep him from smashing his head open on the porcelain if I had to keep him held up in the shower. Maybe when he's a bit stronger. I wonder how many favours I'd owe Parish to make that happen?

I try to be quick about it. I'm just as eager to get back to Blue as I'm sure he is to have me. I throw on Jos's clothes and rejoin him.

"Hey," he says to me first, scooting over so I can climb in.

"See? Came back, didn't I?"

His head practically falls into my neck. I kiss his head and take his hand in mine.

"I got'ch'ya," I tell him softly.

"Blanky?"

"Yeah?"

"Are we going to be okay?"

"We're going to be just fine. I promise."

I lean him down, his head in the crook of my arm. He's staring up at me with those clear blue eyes. "God, I've missed you," I whisper to him. He's just staring. I feel his chest rising higher at each breath. I kiss him deeply. He trembles in my arms as my tongue gently caresses his bottom lip. I go slow, but I manage to coax his mouth open. His whole body tenses as our tongues embrace. I just let him have a little. I pull back slowly, allowing my wetted lips to trace a line down his chin, down his neck. He has grabbed my shoulders, digging his fingers in, but not trying to stop me. I pull myself back up, "It's alright," I whisper to him. I crawl off of the bed.

"Where're you going?" he asks nervously.

I grin. "Nowhere." I grab a curtain and draw it closed. Tonight I just want him to know how much I love him. It has taken us far too long to be this close. I can tell that he's been waiting for this too. We untie his gown, and then I just let him lay there. There isn't an inch of him that I don't attend to. He trembles, holds his breath, moans, breathes heavy again. I don't say a word, but I can tell he's feeling it course through him. He feels me. I'm doing things I've never done before, but they feel right. Everything I've ever imagined, ever dreamt of, and somehow not having it being done to me feels all the better. I am his. All of me is his. I follow his quivering, his pulsing; I taste all of it, all of him.

Then he says it. Trembling, moaning, heart racing, he says it.

"I love you."

I love you too. I will say it, but not now. Now I just want him to feel it. I just want to feel him. When he finally releases, shaking, hyperventilating, I do it.

"I love you, Zac."

I think Doctor Parish finally realizes that he can't keep Blue and me apart, and not even because I'm insistent about it. If anything, I'm totally willing to be put away if it means that I get just these few hours with him, but Blue, he's a mean little bugger when left on his own. And the stronger he gets, the worse he's becoming. I find it funny because I know he's just trying to get his way, but I also know that there's no stopping him from getting his way. For as difficult as Parish thought I was, he was *not* prepared for Blue. There's a reason why alarms used to go off for this kid. Now to prevent alarms from going off, Parish has no choice but to keep me upstairs with him. I'm officially the Blue babysitter. I don't mind at all.

Parish has been running around all over the place, meetings and drop-ins, trying to get me cleared out of the Zero Block. The only case he has for keeping me is for helping him advance his research on his rare specimen. By keeping Blue calm, I help him become a better test subject. Of course, Parish's only interest is prolonging Blue's healthy state, but he has kept some pretty impressive records about the genetic implications of a few experimental treatments. Parish is a genius. Basically by considering Blue a life-long study, he gets full control over him. I'm the tricky part. I'm the part that doesn't really seem medically necessary. There is really only one hope for me.

"Hey, Bathtub."

Parish continues our arrangements with Beth's caregiver. He keeps records of all of our interactions, including a few quick check-ups. Even her own physician can't argue that her anxiety levels decrease more and more with every visit I pay her. It isn't much, but Parish is hopeful that this will help my case. I don't mind. I enjoy doing it. Playing with the kids is the best job in the world. I would think that this has to at least partially clear my name as a runaway. Obviously if I'm still here and helping other kids feel better about being stuck in here, I should be considered an anti-runaway.

Blue isn't quite as supportive of it. The first time he asked me what I was doing and I told him all about it, all he could focus on was, "A girl?" It's funnier because he's so serious as he says it.

"Yeah, a girl. A pretty one, too," I tease.

He does not look happy at all.

"She's also about ten," I add.

Blue visibly relaxes a bit.

"Nothing to worry about," I remind him. "Just keeping an eye on her before she transitions over. Won't be long now. I'm hoping she'll be able to find some familiar faces."

"If not," Blue jumps in, "Froggy and Bear would step in. They're good for that."

"Yeah, they are," I say. Froggy would without a doubt. I've seen firsthand how he handled the Skid that came in. Bear, who knows. He's a good guy, a great guy, but he's so bent on finding his —

"Holy crap!"

"What? What's wrong?"

I replay it in my head. That night with Bear, sitting vigil over Blue's sickbed.

"Cross," I repeat out loud.

"You're scaring me a little here," Blue says.

"DOC!"

Parish comes running like someone has died, and the way I'm running towards him probably convinces him of that as well.

"You have access to records, right?" I'm not asking, I'm demanding.

"What's happened?" He's not following me.

"Beth. Elizabeth Cross. You'd know who her parents are, wouldn't you?"

I can't tell if he's angry with me for causing him such a panic or just thinking really hard.

"They would be on file. Medical history."

"Bear — I mean, I think I know who her father is. Could you tell me?"

Now he's just confused.

"I need to know. It's important."

I can see that he's getting frustrated. He's the kind of guy who calls the shots; having some kid giving orders isn't flying with him very well. All I can do is hope that he trusts me enough.

"Why does she concern you so much? And what good would it do you? If the records are here, they'd be meaningless to you. It's a medical matter. That's all."

"You've spent thirty years searching for your family. A friend of mine's spent ten. He was thrown in here because he got a girl pregnant. He's been dreaming about his kid forever. If it's her, you gotta tell him. He deserves to know."

Parish sighs. "What makes you think that the two are connected?"

"Cross. His girlfriend. And Beth is the right age. Bear... Elijah, his name is Elijah. Elijah Dean. Can you look it up?"

He sighs again. "What's her – "

"0-0-5-0-0-9-1-2-2."

He has me repeat it when he's ready to input it. He doesn't say anything. When it comes up, he hands me the tablet.

Cross, Rachel. Dean, Elijah.

"She's his. She's Bear's."

I know what I want, I know what I want to do, but I can't ask Parish for it. I've already asked for so much. He's saved Blue. He's brought Blue back to me and he's doing everything within his power to keep us together. I owe him everything.

I try to talk myself out of it. I try to tell myself that things will work out on their own.

It haunts me every time I see her.

13

NEW SCENERY

Blue gets better. He's walking around, though often when I get back to the room I find him rolling around in Parish's desk chair, driving him completely around the bend.

"Deal with this!" Parish barks at me.

I laugh and play defense. I'm sure wrestling his patient to the ground isn't quite what he had in mind, but it's Blue's pent-up energy that's working against him. Blue's a Jack-Russell, he needs to run, jump and dig.

It takes some doing, but Parish finally gets my suggestion approved. This time I take him with me.

Blue is less excited than I thought he'd be. He was certainly glad to be getting out of Parish's room, but I had forgotten that this isn't too much of a change of scenery for him. He holds my hand tightly as we walk through the halls of the kids' ward.

"Look familiar?" I ask him.

He shakes his head. "It's painted funny. Doesn't look right." He is genuinely put-off by this. He does not like it at all. I try really hard not to laugh at him. The paint is bright, friendly. It's far more inviting than any other floor I've been on yet. Maybe that's why he mistrusts it so much; he doesn't like it looking friendly.

We meet the kids outside. Blue closes his eyes the moment he feels the sun on his face. He would lie in the sun forever if he could.

The kids notice Blue right away. I've grown so used to him that I have actually forgotten how strange he must seem to them. They stand off, staring, trying to figure out what he is. The only one not afraid to come near us is Bathtub. Beth runs to me as she always does. I'm not even sure if she has taken so much as a second glance at who I've brought with me. I pull her up into my arms, squeezing her tightly.

"I want you to meet someone," I tell her.

She holds my hand, but she isn't afraid. Blue's not much bigger than I am. He looks a little more serious with his hair so short, but he's still a goofball through and through.

"You're not really *all* that blue," she tells him. She isn't disappointed though – I told her the truth about him.

She smiles and tugs at his arm until she can skip off excitedly, dragging him behind her. She's adopted him right away, announcing to everyone that he's "the Blue Man."

I've never seen Blue look so out of place. I would have thought that being surrounded by little versions of him would have thrilled him. As I watch him, I realize that he's feeling pressured into being the grown-up in this situation; it doesn't suit him at all. I have no choice. I run in. I start picking up the ones who are most comfortable around me, capturing them and holding them prisoner in one of their play-forts. Beth nominates herself as the hero. She dubs Blue as her sidekick. Now it's easy.

"You are no match for me!" I boast villainously.

Beth calls the others into an attack, and before I know it, I have at least five of them on me, trying to get me down on the ground, the whole while Blue is egging them on.

"How do you keep up with them all?" Blue asks me as we head back inside.

I laugh. "I keep up with you, don't I?"

He takes my hand and pulls my arm up over his shoulder.

"So that's Bear's kid." He isn't asking. He's contemplating. I've told him everything. He knows exactly what I've been thinking. "You're crazy, you know that, right?"

"Yeah, I know."

Parish tells me more-or-less the same thing. It's a tough sell, but I know that I'm running out of time.

"You said that the only reason you were keeping such a close eye on me was because of Jos," I remind him. "You said that Jos only ever cared about one thing. Maybe that was me, but I'm not so deluded to believe that would be it now. What I do know is that he told me that he believed in doing something good, something right. He wanted to know that someone good, someone who was worthy of a real life, could make it out. He knew that any hope of changing things had to come from the inside. That's why he came. That's why he worked so hard. He had plans lined up, probably years in advance. You can't tell me that you weren't *that* dedicated when you came here. If it were possible, wouldn't you have gotten your sister out? Her son? Didn't you have a plan in place? Some crazy scheme stuffed up your sleeve because you were so certain that it needed to be done? That even if it was just one person, it would make the world that much better?"

"It's not that simple."

"Of course not. Wouldn't be worth doing if it were. Wouldn't *have* to do it if it were easy. But that's what makes it worth it, isn't it? That's what makes everything else seem okay, doesn't it? Just this one. Just this once."

"You understand what this would mean? What would happen if someone discovered that I was involved?"

"But you wouldn't be. It wouldn't be you at all."

"And you understand what this would mean for you? You could never see him again. Never make any form of contact. You would never know what became of him, if he could even make it out there. His medical records, his treatments, they would be locked in here, inaccessible beyond these walls. Yours already is inescapably a life sentence. Any hope you'd have of getting out, of following your own plan, it would be gone. This is something that could only work once. You won't be able to save any of the others."

"I wouldn't say that," I reply with a grin. "It's like you said, I'm here forever. Forever is an awfully long time. I could do a lot of things in forever."

"I'm sure if anyone could, you would be the one to find a way."

"You know it. So can I count on your help?"

"I'm sorry, Dotan. I can't play a part in this."

It was a lot to ask.

"All I can do is a phone call. Just one. Be sure that this is the one you want me to make."

I thank him. It's more than I could ever achieve on my own.

I feel dirtier putting on the clean black jumpsuit than anything I've ever had to slide into in Zero Block. Blue tells me that I look okay, but it doesn't feel right. I button up the front flap which hides the zipper underneath. It makes it look like I've got a coat on overtop of this thing. Blue hands me the hat, the felt beret. I put it on but the moment I see my reflection in the mirror, I hate myself. He comes up behind me and fixes the collar. Even folded down the collar comes up so high that you can't see the barcode hiding back there. It's my third day wearing one of these uniforms. I feel like a traitor even if I haven't done anything yet. Blue has been surprisingly good about it. I thought for sure that he would be the first one to take a jab at me, but in this case he's remained the positive one between us.

"Have fun terrorising everyone, Honey," Blue jokes.

I punch his arm. He whimpers but I know he isn't *that* fragile. Parish wants to wait a little bit longer before letting the board put Blue up for assignment, but we both know that the guy is getting restless being cooped up inside all day. His "Permitted" badge lets him go up and down to the common areas for workers – cafeteria, workout room, indoor garden – but he gets bored by himself. We're the youngest ones to live in the apartments and I think Blue feels more self-conscious about that than about his not-so-normal appearance, which is why *I* think people keep on staring.

The apartment is a decent size. It's bigger than the quad we used to share, and for the first time in his life we actually have a bedroom that isn't a foot away from the entrance. Parish might have cringed at the thought of us sharing a place, but it actually made the arrangement easier. As far as the board is concerned, we're roommates. It's not like they come in to see if we've kept the beds apart or anything. I doubt they'd care much even if they did waltz in unexpectedly. Freak babies aren't exactly something they need to worry about with us.

"You gonna be okay?" I ask him.

"Me? Yeah, of course. I've only got one thing to worry about today," he says.

"Listen, you don't have to –"

"Just don't get caught," he tells me.

I smile. "Guess I'm not so good at that part," I admit. "Haven't gotten away with anything yet."

"It should be me going up there."

I kiss him.

"You're dead, remember?"

He brushes me off. "*Pfft. Dead.* Never stopped me before."

His kisses me one last time then wishes me luck. He won't know if it's worked until I get back in. If he goes to bed alone tonight, he'll know that it didn't.

I scan myself through the elevator and then slip on my black gloves. I'm still not used to scanning with my ID card. It just seems easier to use my branded wrists.

I have to cross to another tower before taking another elevator up to my old ward. There's something about being in this uniform that even catches the attention of White Coats and businesspeople. As a Freak, you might as well be lower than dirt, a cockroach on the floor that no one wants to admit is there. As an attendant, everyone's waiting to see if I'm going to do something. My uniform represents maintaining order, so wherever I go it must mean that there is some form of disorder for me to deal with.

There are a few of us ready to pile into the elevator. Only three other attendants come to the same floor as me. I was lucky in my placement. I get hall duty for the first half then rec-room after dinner. We eat before the inmates do. We are given one hour within a two hour period, switching off to make sure that there are always at least two people at the main posts.

I feel ridiculous, though it gives me some perspective into how I used to view attendants. It was easy to ignore them for the most part, and it always seemed like they would prefer to ignore us. I guess it's true to a point. Seeing people I recognize, even people that I don't but knowing that if I were still here I could know them as people, and trying so hard not to be recognized by them, not wanting to have to explain everything that's happened, knowing that I couldn't even if I wanted to. No wonder they never wanted to make eye-contact with us. I don't want to make eye-contact with them either.

The day seems like it's snailing by. I just keep playing the conversation that I know is coming over and over again. I've imagined so many possible reactions that I can't say which one I actually expect to take place. The one thing I'm fearing the most is that all of this has been a waste of time and effort. Very few people would be willing to do something this crazy. Anything I do or say could ruin everything. If nothing else, I've got to make it back. Blue's counting on me.

I wait in the rec-room, waiting for those quick eaters to start piling in. I know I'll have at least another hour to keep myself company with my own thoughts. Probably two if he's chatty today. He always used to be. Who knows what he's like now. If there's been a new batch of Skids in, he's probably completely beside himself.

It seems to take forever. When the crowds get thick, I scan every face that passes me. I don't want to miss him. I can't miss him.

The big guy's hard to miss. He walks straight towards me, as I knew he would, not even noticing that I'm even there as he goes through the threshold and into the workout room. I stop him. It doesn't take much. Just putting a hand out so that it hits his hip is enough to make me materialize in front of him. I turn the corner and go in with him.

He's staring, but he's not saying anything. His mouth has fallen open; he's recognized me.

I put my finger to my lips to keep him quiet. I tilt my head towards the door. He takes the hint and shuts it.

"We don't have much time," I tell him.

I can tell that I've already just thrown the pieces of his shattered world up in the air and I haven't even told him anything yet.

"Blanky? What the... You're one of *them* now?"

"Trust me, least important detail right now," I tell him. "Bear, I've found her."

I can see the wheels turning, but I don't know how fast.

"Your daughter. I've found her."

Those shattered pieces have just been obliterated by an atom bomb. He's going to pass out. He stretches his arm out, trying to grab hold of the wall. I help him towards it.

"Are you sure?" he finally says.

"Wouldn't be here if I wasn't. She's an amazing kid. You'll love her, Bear. You'll be so proud of her."

He's shaking now. His whole face is flushed. His eyes are turning red.

"Her name's Beth. Elizabeth Cross."

He can't hold it in anymore. Every orifice in his face is leaking. He has his arms crossed over his body, trying to hold himself together; he's keeling over. He's spurting out sobbing laughs. It takes him a few to find his words again.

"C-Can I see her?" he pleads.

"That's the plan," I say, using Blue's faithful grin as my own.

I slip him the stuff he needs. My instructions are brief, but I tell him to wait until I'm done my shift. I can't get him out with me, but I can get him into a stairwell.

When I come out of my shift in the rec-room, I see him

waiting along the wall in the hallway. We're all heading towards the elevators. No one takes much notice of him. There's no curfew. He can stay up as late as he wants. The hallway is public space. With how red his face is, it wouldn't be wrong to guess that he needs some time alone.

I told him to wait until we clear out. If I'm in the elevator with a bunch of others, they won't need to rely on me to be scanned in. I keep my hands shoved deep inside my pockets and try to look exhausted – it isn't that hard to do when you're this anxious. No one should take much notice of my missing gloves. With my ID card and gloves to cover his codes, Bear should be able to get into the stairwell with little issue. Yes, there are cameras, but no one will check them thoroughly until something has gone wrong. Parish should already be altering the system. Bear's clean slate of health makes him an ideal candidate for alternative treatment. Parish reassured me that it's easier to fall through the cracks during a transition. His Doc will expect him to be with someone else, and no one else will be expecting to receive him. Numbers moved down to Zero Block are rarely checked up on. It's quite a long-term commitment for Parish to keep putting in false updates, but he's confident that in a year or two, it will be easy to eliminate him from the system altogether.

I'm nervous. I know he'll be okay. Blue. He's supposed to be waiting in the stairwell. As far as Parish is aware, I'm the one sneaking back into the stairwell. Blue and I both knew how well that would work.

e's gone in. Smuggling Bear a jacket is easy; he's far closer to Jos's size than either Blue or I, and Parish now has no use for his son's clothes. All I have to do is move to my next position. Once we're on the third floor we can take the bridge over to the other tower. I've got a pick-up to make on the ground floor, so I head down. I hope that Bear's made it this far. With my ID he should have been able to scan himself out. With Blue's ID on, he should be able to walk straight through without too many concerns.

I see him. He's wearing Jos's clothes. Blue found him

alright. I just have to hope that he got out alright too. Bear has made good time. I've never seen him look so scared.

"Got them?" I ask.

He reaches inside his jacket.

"Good," I say. "The cards?"

He unclips the one he has on his jacket and hands both Blue's and mine over.

"Let's get you processed," I say with a smile.

He grabs my arm. "What if it doesn't work? What if they find out?"

I squeeze his arm a little. "And what if it *does*? Keep focused on that. Let me worry about the other."

We head to processing. This is where he's on his own. I show him the desk. The rest is up to him.

I go through the staff door. I'm on the inside and can see and hear everything going on at the main reception desk. I stand to the side, waiting for instructions. It was only fitting that I be called to help Beth with her new transition.

"*Parish*, is it?" the woman asks.

Bear nods nervously and finally spits out a "yes."

"Just sign here, please."

His hand is shaking so bad, I can see it from here, but it's alright, he gets it done.

"Just a moment please, Sir."

He stares right at me. I instantly look away and hope he gets the hint.

He has all of his documents laid out over the table top. Everything, thanks to Dr. Parish, made ready to go. He had to copy over most of his own son's records, duplicating what he needed to, but it should hopefully be enough.

The front desk woman finishes scanning what she needs into the computer and looks up at him. He's frozen. He's noticed at the same time I have that his jacket sleeve is bunched up just enough to show some of his wrist. I'm frozen too.

"Everything looks in order," she says without a hitch.

The tension in me rushes out like a race horse. She didn't

even see it. Bear pulls his sleeve down under the desk as she jabbers on about expectations and resources for the fostering.

I'm given the go ahead. I have to hand it to Parish, even though Bear might have just been struck with all of this today, as far as the Institution is aware, "Elijah Parish" has started this application process weeks ago, including interviews. It didn't take as much coaxing as I thought it would. When Parish explained the situation to his son, he jumped on board. Probably the first time that those two have ever agreed on anything.

I enter one of the little white rooms. Poor thing is sitting nervously in a big chair, swinging her legs, staring at the floor. I can't blame her. The news would have been shocking, especially for a kid who has never known anything else. She's never met this new family. I can just imagine all of the questions she must have running through her head. I am so glad that I get to be the one to see her out. This needed to be me.

I don't speak too loudly. "Hey, Bathtub."

She looks up and her whole face changes.

I kneel down with my arms out. She jumps right in. Her tiny arms squeeze around my neck a little too hard, but that's okay.

"Do I get to go home with you?"

I can't help but smile. "Not this time. But you have to trust me on this one, okay? You trust me?"

I pull her in front of me so that we can do this properly. It's important that we see each other eye to eye.

She nods her head.

"I found you the greatest dad in the whole wide world. And I promise you that he's going to spoil you, and love you like crazy. I'd trust him with my life. And I wouldn't let anyone else take you, because you deserve the best there is, right?"

I can see that she's still nervous. I give her one more hug. "Hey, I won't let anything bad happen to you. And that guy out there, he knows it. He's going to take really good care of you. I promise."

She nods her head. "You really picked him out just for me?" she asks.

I rub her head playfully. "Specially for you!"

She pats her messed hair back down, and I hold my hand out for her to take. Her little hand wraps tightly around two of my fingers. She's as ready as she'll ever be. I'm just hoping that *he* is.

As I come into view from the reception desk, I can see that Bear is completely fixated on me. He's still frozen into place as I come through the staff door.

I stop once it closes behind me, Beth and I still hand-in-hand. I'm sure that Bear has forgotten that I'm even alive. He wants to cry; I can see how hard he's fighting it back.

"All yours," I tell him.

I loosen my hand and let her walk forward on her own. Bear kneels now.

"Hello, Sir," she says politely. "My name is Elizabeth, but he calls me Bathtub."

Bear spits out a chuckle, but it releases the floodgate of tears that he was holding back.

I hate to break-up their reunion, but we aren't out of the clear yet. "Hey, we gotta make tracks," I say to him. Then I turn to Beth, "I need you to take his hand, now, okay?"

She follows my instruction, and Bear tries to walk upright despite his bleary eyes. I give a nod to reception as I take these two to the main door, just to keep them moving. I can't leave, and I know that eyes will be watching me to make sure that I don't. The sleepy man in the booth will have to buzz him out.

"Your car is just around the corner. You'll know it when you see it. Take care," I say and then start to back away before either of us start to make a scene out of it.

I stand back and let them both go. As soon as they're out the door I turn and run. I go straight for the stairs, racing up them like my life depends on it. I charge into my apartment, letting the door close itself behind me in its own good time. I jump over any little thing that's in front of me, and get to the balcony door. It's only a few feet of space, but I can see the car from here. Jos is standing on the outside, leaning against it. The Institution wall is too high, I don't see Bear until he crosses the street. There he is – the sweetest little girl keeping pace at his side. Jos greets him and opens up the back door. Jos looks over. He looks up. I wave at him. He gives me a quick short wave, only a formal transaction. I can't fault him for that.

I feel his arms around me. I feel him kiss the back of my neck.

"You made it," I say to Blue softly.

"So did you."

I lace my fingers through his.

I watch Jos get in. It's a quiet road. It doesn't take long once the car is started up for it to make good distance. Blue watches it disappear with me.

"You did good today," he tells me.

I pull him in front of me and hold him close. He tucks his head under my chin.

"About time, isn't it?"

14

ONE LAST PIECE

Parish keeps his distance from us for a few weeks. I'm sure he has more than his hands full with all of the trouble I've caused him. Blue's the first one to interact with him at all; it's just a check-up. He's doing fine but Parish is still putting off getting him placed. I won't argue with the man. I won't argue with him about anything.

Then *I* get called in. He doesn't even meet me at his office. I'm paged by my barcode number to go to a floor I've never been on. I find my way to the clinic. I still appreciate those maps that pop up when I scan in while on task. I'm in my uniform so no one stands in my way, though I'm sure at least one of these guys thinks it's strange to have a lone attendant roaming around. I feel like I'm in just another ward like mine, but I haven't come across too many young faces. I try not to look at them. I'm already invading their space.

I get to the clinic desk and announce that I've come in. She pages Parish and lets me come behind the desk.

"Ah," is all Parish says when he appears. Somehow that's supposed to explain everything. I guess in a way it does, I don't even think about it, I automatically start following him. He has me well trained after all.

"What's up, Doc?" I ask when we're out of sight from the

lobby.

He's quiet for a few more steps, and then stops. He faces me with his lips slightly apart as if he's calculating something. It isn't more than a second later that he speaks, more so in my general direction than to me. "A few years back I met a strange boy who, for no reason at all, told me to keep an eye out for someone he had no memory of."

I have no words. I know this story.

"With all that's happened in these past few months, it never really seemed like the most appropriate time. I never really asked you about it. If I gave you the opportunity – "

"Now?" I interrupt.

"He's here," he says. "I've been treating him for six years now."

"Does he know?"

"I wasn't sure how you wanted me to tell him."

I feel my stomach caught in my throat. I nod. It's all I can do.

Parish takes me to a small examination room. A man is sitting up on the bed complacently. He's nothing like I pictured. He's a thinner man, short, longish curled hair, short black beard, thick eyebrows.

"Mornin', Doc," he says.

"Mr. Abbott," Parish greets.

"Have I done something?" he asks, laughing a little. "Who's the kid?"

Parish looks to me. I can't. I can't do it. I may not be a parent, and I probably never will be one, but if I've learned anything from Parish, even from Bear, it's that a father's worst fear is knowing that *this* is where his kid is. Maybe I'm doing alright now, but who really wants to know what I faced to get here?

"Shepherd," I say. "Zacchaeus Shepherd."

Parish doesn't even blink an eye against me.

"Hm," my father says. "Hard to believe that I have a son about your age."

"Is that so?" I say.

He chokes out an awkward laugh. "So, you've come to take me away?"

"Not as such," Parish interjects. "Mr... *Shepherd* here represents a pilot project of mine. He's trained in patient consultation and has so far proven to be very effective. I thought he might be beneficial in reducing your blood pressure. At your age, Mr. Abbott a simple thing like that can have rather detrimental effects, even potentially fatal under the right conditions."

He laughs. "So what? Is he going to rub my shoulders and tell me a bedtime story?"

"I don't believe so," Parish says coolly. "He charges extra for that."

The eruption of laughter that bursts out of him is so pure, so infectious.

"You're done with me for today, Mr. Abbott," Parish says when his patient has calmed down a little. "I would, however, prescribe a short walk."

"Alright. Alright. You're the doctor." He stands up and claps me hard on the back. He's barely an inch taller than me. "Let's go, Shepherd."

I stumble awkwardly along.

"So..." I begin, "...you said you have a son?"

"It's a long story," he says pleasantly.

"I think I have time for a long walk," I reply.

He laughs at that, claps me on my back again, and tells me, "You're alright, kid. You're alright."

I smile. *Yes, I think I am.*

ACKNOWLEDGEMENTS

It's taken a few years and a large team to bring *Parish* out into the world. Thank you to everyone who supported this project from the beginning of *Freakhouse* to the final Kickstarter campaign!

A big thank you to my Ninja Readers, Tiffany, MacKenzie, and Joann, and to Shaunta for bringing us together!

To Squirrely, who can finally put this book down.

And to those family, friends, and friendly strangers who generously contributed to the *Parish* project:

Jay Ross, Joe Main, My big brother, Tammy and JR Johnston, Moira McLaughlin, Esmee Maltby, Kerry-Anne O'Connor, Lindsey Rojem, Kelsey Theobald, Alex Koshynsky, Josh Snofsky, Gareth Loyd, and Lisa Cheryba.

Thank you all!

ABOUT THE AUTHOR

Ashley Newell is a Canadian fiction author. She holds a BA in English Literature and Classical Studies from the University of British Columbia, a BEd from the University of Calgary, and a few stray credits from Queens University's Bader International Study Centre in Herstmonceux, UK. She is a creative writing mentor, and an avid supporter of the NaNoWriMo challenge. She currently resides in Calgary with her husband, son, and mischievous dog.

NOVELS BY ASHLEY NEWELL

Galen
Freakhouse
Parish: a sequel to Freakhouse

Visit www.newellbooks.com for more about this author.

Made in the USA
Columbia, SC
20 May 2017